CORE'S ATTACK

COSMOS' GATEWAY BOOK 6

S.E. SMITH

MONTANA
PUBLISHING

CONTENTS

ACKNOWLEDGMENTS

I would like to thank my husband Steve for believing in me and being proud enough of me to give me the courage to follow my dream. I would also like to give a special thank you to my sister and best friend, Linda, who not only encouraged me to write, but who also read the manuscript. Also to my other friends who believe in me: Julie, Jackie, Christel, Sally, Jolanda, Lisa, Laurelle, Debbie, and Narelle. The girls that keep me going!

And a special thanks to Paul Heitsch, David Brenin, Samantha Cook, Suzanne Elise Freeman, and PJ Ochlan—the awesome voices behind my audiobooks!

—S.E. Smith

Montana Publishing
Science Fiction Romance
CORE'S ATTACK: COSMOS' GATEWAY BOOK 6

First E-Book Published December 2018
Cover Design by Melody Simmons

Summary: From the moment Core met Avery, he was captivated by the human woman who shields herself with an icy demeanor and a gun....

ISBN: (KDP Paperback) 9781791898946
ISBN: (Independent Paperback) 9781944125608
ISBN: (eBook) 9781944125592

Published in the United States by Montana Publishing.

{1. Romance—Fiction. 2. Science Fiction Romance—Fiction. 3. Paranormal Romance—Fiction. 4. Urban Fantasy—Fiction.—5. Contemporary Fantasy}

www.montanapublishinghouse.com

SYNOPSIS

Thrust into a deadly game....

Avery Lennox has been called many names, but bond mate was never one of them. Her position as Chief Security Officer for Cosmos Raines guarantees that her life will never be boring—especially after her genius boss decides to open a portal between Earth and Baade, a world filled with an annoying, male-dominated species called Prime —but after meeting one particular alien, Avery decides to pursue him through the portal.

The trip to another world was...indescribable, but it's when she returns home that Avery is in the most danger. Someone else is as fascinated with Core as she is, and believes Avery is the perfect bait.

From the moment Core Ta'Duran met Avery, he was captivated by the human woman who shields herself with an icy demeanor and a gun. Avery knows he wants a lifetime with her, and even though she is fighting their bond, she still appears on his world with a tantalizing offer: three days together with no questions, no ties, and no regrets.

When he follows her back to Earth, instead of finding Avery, he discovers a menacing message left for him: *agree to be hunted or Avery dies.*

Can Avery and Core turn the tables on the ruthless killer who wants to display Core as a trophy in his private collection, or will Core lose the most crucial battle of his life?

CAST OF CHARACTERS

Characters' Relationships:
Teriff, Leader of Baade - **mated to** Tresa:
four sons, J'kar, Borj, Mak, and Derik and one daughter, Terra
Angus and Tilly Bell, humans—**married**:
three daughters, Hannah, Tansy, and Tink

Warriors of Baade: Ruling family:
J'kar 'Tag Krell Manok **mated to** Jasmine 'Tinker' Bell:
twin daughters, Wendy and Tessa
Borj 'Tag Krell Manok **mated to** Hannah Bell:
twin boy & girl, Sky and Ocean
Mak 'Tag Krell Manok **mated to** Tansy Bell:
twin daughters, Sonya and Mackenzie
Terra 'Tag Krell Manok **mated to** Cosmos Raines
Derik 'Tag Krell Manok **mated to** Amelia Thomas aka Runt

Members of Cosmos' Security Team:
GarrettAvery Lennox
Trudy WilsonRose Caine
Rico GarciaMaria Garcia

Amelia 'Runt' Thomas

Prime Warriors of Baade:
Core Ta'Duran **mated to** Avery Lennox
Merrick Ta'Duran, Eastern Clan Leader, **mated to** Addie Banks
Hendrik, Northern Clan Leader, **mated to** Trudy Wilson
RITA (Earth) **zapped by** FRED
RITA2 (Baade) **zapped by** DAR

Eastern Clan:
Nadine Ta'Duran - Core's younger sister
Nadu Ta'Duran - Core's mother
Trainer Ta'Duran - Core's father

Humans:
Karl Markham: Assassin/Mercenary for hire/older half-brother to Weston Wright.
Weston Wright: Assassin/Mercenary/half-brother to Karl Markham.
Priscilla Housing: Mother of Karl and Weston
Afon Dolinski: Former right-hand man to Boris Avilov
Boris Avilov: Russian Mafia boss
Richmond Albertson: Secretary of State
Askew Thomas: President of the United States
Markham's soldiers: Owens, Carter, Grant, and Bradley
Walt: Markham's Pilot
Rex: CRI's pilot
Doughboy: Hacker
Robert: Avery's driver
Carol: Hostess on CRI's corporate jet

PROLOGUE

Twenty years ago:

"Avery, do you remember what we told you?" Donna Lennox asked, brushing loose strands of brown hair back from her face.

Twelve-year-old Avery Lennox nodded, her face devoid of expression. She didn't want her parents to know how scared she was or that she had any doubts. Returning her mother's intense gaze, she lifted her chin.

"Never hesitate. Make a decision and follow through with it. Double check your surroundings. Move with precision, and never let your foe know that you are scared," she repeated.

"That's right," her father said with a proud smile. "Don't allow yourself to be distracted by anything other than your mission."

"I won't," Avery promised.

"Good luck, sweetheart. We know you'll do the best you can," her mother added, giving her a hug.

Avery allowed herself to enjoy her mom's embrace for a moment, then gripped the ball in her hands and ran out onto the field. Dropping the soccer ball to the ground, she executed the moves she and her dad had been practicing. Three girls ran over to join her, and Avery ruthlessly pushed down her nervousness.

She was in another new city with new kids, a new school, and a new home. Her parents did the best they could to give her a normal life. Playing sports was one of their concessions.

For the next two hours, Avery focused on her mission: kicking the other team's butt... without being too greedy about it. By the end of the last quarter, she was glowing, and the other girls on her team were energized by the six-point lead.

When the final whistle blew, Avery turned to her parents with a huge grin and lifted her arms up victoriously. Her team surrounded her, but Avery's shining eyes were on the grinning faces of her parents. She turned when her teammate Kassy called her name.

Kassy's eyes widened with shock when Avery suddenly jerked and stumbled into her, the glimmer of excitement fading as Avery felt something warm and wet seeping through the fingers of her left hand as it touched her side.

She looked down, and her legs trembled as she noticed the bright red blood saturating her shirt. The numbness was giving way to intense, burning pain. Avery distantly noted the screams that filled the air as Kassy's fist clenched around the fabric of Avery's long-sleeved soccer jersey and the girl's weight pulled them both to the ground.

"Get down! Get down! Shooter! Everyone, GET DOWN!"

Avery rolled onto her back, pressing her hand against the wound in her side the way her mom had taught her to do if she didn't have anything else to apply pressure with. She could hear screams, yelling, and sirens wailing, an odd cacophony against the stillness of the blue sky above her. She turned her head toward the bleachers where her parents had been watching her play.

They were the only ones still on the bleachers. She knew it was them by their matching black coats. Her father's upper body was leaning awkwardly against the seat behind him. Her mother struggled to push herself up from where she was lying on the plank between two rows of seats.

Avery's eyes followed the man walking toward her parents. Unlike everyone else, he didn't appear alarmed. She took in every detail of his features: his exclusive, name-brand sunglasses; the thin scar on his clean-shaven jaw; his black hair and high cheekbones; the European cut of his clothing; and his Italian-made shoes, possibly size eleven. He wasn't American. His left ring finger glinted with a gold ring—not a wedding ring—it was decorated with the head of a lion with red ruby eyes—no, not a lion—an intricate series of connecting circles —infinity.

The man paused by her father and aimed his gun. The barrel looked funny. Silencer—9mm handgun.

A silencer is used to reduce sound intensity and minimize flash by cooling the propellant gases, she remembered.

The man turned the weapon toward her mother. He said something to her mom. Avery followed the motion of his lips, picking out several words—spoken in a language she was still learning: Croatian. She mentally put together the pieces she understood to find the meaning of his speech—*betrayal comes with a price. You should not have had a child. She led me straight to you.*

Her mother turned her head and looked at Avery, her eyes flashing with pain, grief, and regret. Avery didn't close her eyes when the man pulled the trigger. She saw her mother's head jerk to the side before her body collapsed back between the seats.

The man turned his head and looked at Avery. She returned his gaze with unblinking eyes devoid of emotion. The man must have thought she was dead because he slid the pistol under his coat and walked away from Avery's murdered parents. The first responders arrived on the scene and no one stopped him as he continued along the nature trail that wound through the park. To them, he was an elegantly dressed foreign businessman, not a rampaging madman.

Leaving her alive would be the man's fatal mistake. Avery was weak and seriously injured, her blood soaking the ground along with Kassy's, but still alive, and she had been studying and memorizing every detail of his appearance. She replayed the incident over and over in her head to make sure she would never forget any critical detail. Someday she would hunt that man down, and when she looked him in the eye during his last moments, she would have no doubt that she was killing the guilty man.

Beside her, Avery heard Kassy's mother hysterically wailing. Two men rushed over to them. Avery tensed, but otherwise remained still as they passed by her and went to Kassy.

"She's gone," the uniformed man leaning over Kassy said.

"No! My baby.... My baby.... Oh, God, no!" Kassy's mother sobbed uncontrollably.

Avery forced herself to remain still when she felt fingers against her throat. The uniformed man leaning over her released a hissing breath. He turned her head and looked into her eyes. She tried not to blink against the blinding light of the sun, but her eyelids slowly lowered.

"This one is still alive! Get the stretcher over here."

"Helicopter ETA one minute."

Overhead, a shadow blocked the sun. For a brief moment, Avery looked into the compassionate eyes of the EMT bending over her. Her lips moved, but no sound came out. Her mind registered that this man's eyes were too compassionate for him to be a cold-blooded killer. Then she remembered the expressions in her parents' eyes and their training.

No, even killers could make you think they cared if they were trained well enough.

A new sound could be heard above the crying. She heard voices in the background, and the man was replaced by a woman. Avery looked into the woman's blue eyes. Now this was what she was expecting to see: distant and detached eyes with no emotion reflected in them.

"Targets?" the woman asked as she took over from the EMT.

"Targets? Oh, you mean victims? This girl and the other one who was standing next to her. The other girl didn't make it. They have her mother over at the ambulance. There was also a man and a woman in the stands," the man continued with a shake of his head. "When will the nut cases just decide to take themselves out instead of innocent bystanders?"

"Load her in the helicopter and alert the hospital that we are transporting one in critical condition and two fatalities," the woman ordered.

"What unit are you with? That looks like a military medevac. Which hospital are you taking her to?" the startled EMT suddenly demanded, growing uneasy.

"The child is under our jurisdiction now," the woman replied.

Avery could feel her body shutting down even as her mind balked at the woman's statement. Danger—she was in danger. The man in black was out there. He would find out she was still alive and come to finish the mission. That was what spies and assassins did when they missed their target.

She needed to stay alert. He would come for her. Her parents were always prepared in case they needed to escape. They had warned her that something like this might happen and that she should always be ready. They had trained her and tried to give her a normal life, but they had lived on the run, always looking over their shoulders—until today. Today, they had been looking at her, and it had gotten them killed.

She was the child they had never wanted to have. They were the lovers who weren't supposed to fall in love for real.

Even as the drugs were administered and her eyes closed, Avery was already formulating a plan. She would escape. There was a safe house. There was always a safe house—for people like herself and her parents.

1

Present Day:

Houston, Texas headquarters of Cosmos Raines Industries

"RITA, did Rose send in the report I asked for?" Avery murmured as she pressed her palm to the security panel to open the door of her office.

"Good evening, Avery. I've loaded the report and it will be on your computer when you log in. How was your day?" RITA asked.

"It went well, thank you. How did Runt do today?" Avery asked as she walked across the room to her desk and placed her small bag and cell phone on the corner.

"She really is such a sweetheart," RITA replied.

Avery paused, her expression as neutral as it had been before Cosmos' weird AI evaded answering her question directly. For a moment, Avery ignored her computer and instead looked out the window. The brilliant, colorful lights of downtown Houston greeted her. She shook her head in disgust. She'd been so absorbed with work that she hadn't realized the sun had set hours ago.

"What did she do today?" Avery asked, her voice laced with a touch of amused resignation.

"Nothing… too dangerous. I believe several villages in India will receive funding to build schools and clinics thanks to the generous donations of a few select individuals," RITA diplomatically explained.

Avery reached up and pinched the bridge of her nose. RITA, the AI computer system behind Cosmos Raines Industries and the brainchild of Tilly Bell and her illustrious employer, Cosmos Raines, sounded far too smug for it to not be important.

Cosmos and Tilly insisted that RITA's name stood for Really Intelligent Technical Assistant. Avery had decided that RITA's name should be changed to Really Irritating Technical Assistant because that is what it felt like after she finished cleaning up the messes that were left behind. Given that Tilly Bell had contributed to RITA's programming, Avery supposed it wasn't all that surprising. Tilly was as brilliant as Cosmos—and had a free-spirit, rosy view of the world despite some of the heartache they had lived through when Hannah was kidnapped and Tansy was almost killed. Cosmos and Tilly had designed RITA to help the people around her and, more often than not, Avery found the AI's help often caused her additional headaches.

Avery blinked and turned when she heard the buzz of her cell phone. A glance at the screen told her that the 'nothing dangerous' was enough to alert the State Department. Taking a deep breath, she counted to ten before picking up the phone and forcing a smile on her lips. Touching the screen, she walked around her desk and sank down into the plush leather chair.

"Secretary Albertson, what a pleasant surprise. How can I help you this evening?" Avery politely asked. She leaned back in her chair as she listened to the blistering rant. "Really? That is fascinating, sir. Yes, I can see why the Indian Minister is very upset…. Yes, sir, I'm sure no one would be happy to discover they've been hacked. It is a growing security issue throughout the world. I believe I read in today's paper that the Minister is currently under investigation. The article stated he has received illegal payouts from certain shell companies that were laundering money…. No, sir, I didn't realize that he was claiming that the companies were legitimate. If I'm not mistaken, several of the companies were under surveillance for trying to do business here in the States.... No, sir, no one from the State or Justice Departments has shared classified information with me. It was in the Times, I believe." Avery fought the urge to cross her eyes as the Secretary of State continued with his tirade. She was going to need a stiff drink by the time he finished. "Yes, of course, anyone would be upset at suddenly losing that much money.... Yes, sir.... Yes, sir, Cosmos does have some business interests in India, but we've never dealt with the Minister. The objective of Cosmos Raines Industries is to focus on education, health, and technology for women in small, rural villages.... No, sir, Cosmos has been out of the country for the past several weeks." Avery silently rolled her eyes at just how far *out of the county* he had been, but smoothly continued. "As head of his security, I would be the first to know if anyone at CRI was involved in hacking a foreign dignitary.... Yes, sir. If I discover any information, I'll be happy to pass it along to you—personally," Avery added, repeating the Secretary's emphasized request. "I hope you have a good evening as well, sir. Good night."

Avery hung up and tossed her cell phone onto her desk. She leaned her head into her hand and released a soft curse. The headache that had been threatening all day now felt like a major wrecking ball battering her brain.

"Nothing dangerous? Ten million dollars, RITA. The Criminal Oligarchs of the world do not like it when someone steals ten million dollars out of their personal piggy bank," Avery groaned.

"Ten million dollars is pocket change to them, Avery," RITA retorted nonchalantly.

"I need you to compile a dossier on the Secretary of State. Something is going on. See if there is any reason for someone to blackmail him—a mistress, an illicit affair, gambling, unusual financial deals—anything that could compromise him," she instructed, lifting her head and looking at her computer screen.

She grimaced when she saw something far more disturbing sitting on the corner of her desk. The life-sized, curvy woman smiled at her.

Avery leaned her head back against the headrest of the chair and closed her eyes.

"Do you know how unsettling it is to know that you can take on a corporeal form now, RITA?" Avery muttered.

"I'm still trying to find the perfect program. Do you think this one makes my butt look big?" RITA asked, sliding off the corner of the desk, turning her back, and looking at Avery with twinkling green eyes over her holographic shoulder.

Avery chuckled and shook her head. "I'm not answering that. The last time I said yes to the question about your boobs, FRED deactivated my ATM card," she tiredly replied, opening her eyes and sitting up. "I think you have a lovely figure."

"I've been telling her the same thing, but she wouldn't believe me," FRED murmured from where he was sitting in one of the plush leather chairs by the electric fireplace.

"I'm being invaded by holographic, horny robots. God, but I need a drink," Avery groaned, rising from her chair and walking around her desk to the small bar.

"No, Avery love, you need a vacation," RITA responded with a sweet smile.

Avery's lips twitched with a mysterious smirk. "I've already scheduled it, as you are well aware," she answered, pouring a small glass of red wine.

"I haven't figured out a way to move things in the physical world yet, but we are working on it. You'll have to see Cosmos for a portal device. He keeps them locked up now—but I happen to know someone who could help you break into the safe," RITA teased.

Avery chuckled. "Playing matchmaker again, RITA?" she asked, turning and raising an eyebrow at the spectral AI figure who was now sitting on the arm of the chair where her 'boyfriend' sat.

"Who me? Of course! You work far too hard, and the job you do is dangerous, Avery. You deserve to be happy, honey," RITA said, sounding so much like Tilly Bell that Avery's gut twisted.

"Thank you, Mother RITA. I think I can manage my own life from here," she dryly responded. "I need you to put a lock on Runt. She is not to hack into any accounts outside of her assigned missions. I'm trying to keep the girl alive. If she keeps going rogue, I'll have to reassign her to a different division."

RITA's expression turned serious. "Amelia won't respond well to a cage, Avery. She might bolt again," she warned.

Avery shot RITA a pointed look. "Make sure that she doesn't. Now, if that is all, I need to review the files on the Avilov case. Did Rose or Trudy find anything on Afon Dolinski?"

"His car was found—underwater. His body has not been recovered. If I didn't know so much about the man, I'd swear he was dead. But—knowing what we do, I have to believe he is still alive," she muttered in irritation.

"Easy, love. I can see your binary coding shimmering," FRED soothed.

Avery lifted a hand and rubbed her brow. FRED was right. Zeros and ones were replacing the formerly smooth image of RITA's golden brown skin. Avery didn't know if RITA was having issues with the stability of the corporeal form program or if there was just a heavy load currently on the CRI's mainframe.

"Mm, I think Amelia is having trouble sleeping and is working late tonight. We might need to keep her company, darling," RITA murmured, turning to FRED.

"Please do," Avery ordered. "If I need anything, I'll contact you."

"Righty-o, love. Come along, darling. I think Amelia is scanning The Bank of Dubai's systems," RITA chuckled.

"If we replicate, I want little AIs just like her," FRED replied as they vanished.

"Replicate—little AIs? Heaven help us all. I really need to talk to Cosmos and Tilly," Avery grumbled.

Returning to her seat, she spoke the login command and leaned forward when the screen came up. She scanned the report, impatiently tapping a pen on her notepad.

"What am I missing?" she murmured, staring at the screen.

As tired as she was, she was too distracted to call it a night. Avery felt guilty and grief-stricken, and as much as she needed to keep that from the others—Cosmos especially—within her own mind, her feelings needed to be dealt with.

It was her duty to protect Cosmos Raines and his family—a duty that she had failed to accomplish. Boris Avilov, a Russian billionaire and head of a Russian mafia group, had murdered Adam Raines, Cosmos' father.

Avilov had wanted Tansy Bell, who was a CPAT operative and a close family friend of Cosmos. Tansy had stolen information from Avilov that made him very unpopular with his comrades. They didn't appreciate the detailed information he had kept on his illicit business dealings with some of the most powerful men in the world—including the Vice President of the United States, whose agenda to get promoted by eliminating his boss was exposed.

Cosmos and a team of alien warriors from a distant world had ruined Avilov's plans to terminate Tansy. Unfortunately, during the mission, one of the aliens—Merrick Ta'Duran—had been captured by Avilov's men along with two Russian policewomen who had been helping Cosmos.

Afterward, Avilov had thought Cosmos would be an easy target. To the outside world, Cosmos was a shy billionaire, a genius inventor who lived in a world of privilege and gadgets. In reality, Cosmos was all of those and a modern-day superhero/superspy who used his wealth and inventions to fight against corruption and crime. Still, none of Cosmos' inventions, gadgets, or their Intel had been enough to protect his parents.

Avery bowed her head and closed her eyes. She knew what Avilov had done to the kind and gentle man. Pushing her chair back, she picked up her drink and walked back over to the window. It was done—there was no way to undo it. Raking herself over the coals for not preventing it was not helpful to anyone.

Staring out over the city again, Avery thought of another reason for her unease. There was a long list of dead bad guys and three missing perps that she wanted to confirm were dead or locked up before she closed the case, yet it wasn't the bad guys that she kept thinking about—it was a tall, dark, and very sexy good guy.

"What makes him different from any other man?" she wondered.

Besides the fact that he is an alien, she thought with a shake of her head.

Although that might have helped pique her curiosity, she hadn't felt the same reaction to any of the other 'Prime warriors' she'd met. No, it was Core Ta'Duran who had done the impossible. He had made her curious and was a constant sexy distraction.

She hadn't even known that aliens existed until after Avilov's people had attacked. While the team was en route to help, RITA had offhandedly said 'By the way, Avery, I guess you should know that Cosmos has created a portal to an alien world. The warehouse is full of them at the moment. Please don't shoot any of them. It could cause an intergalactic incident.'

Fortunately, her handpicked team had accepted the revelation as just a routine part of another mission. Avery wasn't sure why she had been shocked that no one had reacted with disbelief. As Jenny, the resident doctor for the team explained, anything was possible when working with Cosmos Raines.

Avery lowered the glass in her hand and narrowed her eyes. Merrick had been found and returned to his world. Perhaps she should check on him. Avery snorted at her excuse to go through the portal and get closer to a certain alien who wasn't Merrick... but she had already scheduled the days off, and this game that she and Core had been playing with each other since their first meeting needed to come to an end.

Finishing her drink, she walked back over to the bar and cleaned the glass. She tidied the area and looked over at the computer. She was starting to feel edgy.

"Three days. I'll give myself three days to get him out of my system," she murmured to herself.

Satisfied with her decision, she walked over to her desk, picked up her phone as she passed by, before she sank into the plush leather chair. She pressed a contact number on the screen, and waited for Cosmos to answer.

"Have you found Dolinski?" Cosmos asked as a way of greeting.

Avery raised an eyebrow.

"Not yet, but I will. I'm calling in my bonus," she stated.

There was a long silence before she heard Cosmos take a deep breath. She smiled. It wasn't often that she caught him off-guard.

"Are you sure about this, Avery? There are—things you don't understand about the Prime," Cosmos muttered.

Avery could picture Cosmos running his fingers through his hair. He did that when his brain was kicking into gear and running through all the relevant scenarios. She looked at the computer screen and swiped her finger across it. She selected a new file titled 'Bonus.' Inside was a report that she had requested from RITA about the Prime, their world, their anatomy, and personal notes that she had added about Core. An image of the man in question filled half of the screen.

Six foot six inches tall, with two hundred and fifty pounds of defined muscle. She sighed softly at the sight. He wore his black hair short. His silver-colored eyes held twin flames that sent a wave of heat through her. The expression on his face was assessing and downright predatory. He was a hunter, and she wanted him.

"You promised, Cosmos. Avilov is dead, only three of his men are still unaccounted for, and the alien has returned to his world. The situation has been contained. Three days is all I'm asking for. After that, you can have the device back and I will finish locating the missing men. Trudy and Rose are working on it, as well. I'll personally lead the team when I return," she stated, staring at Core's image.

"It's not that, Avery. I... Listen, I just don't want you to get hurt," Cosmos admitted in a rough voice.

"You don't have to worry about that, Cosmos," she reassured him.

There was another pause before Cosmos spoke again. "I'll leave a gateway device on the desk in my lab. RITA will let you in and program it with RITA2's help. I hope to god you know what you are doing, Avery. If you are Core's bond mate, your lives will be forever connected whether you want them to be or not," he warned.

"I don't believe in magic, Cosmos. I'll be there tomorrow. Thank you," she replied before disconnecting the call.

She leaned back in her seat. As much as she hated the idea of moving on, it might be time to find another position when she returned. She had been with CRI for six years. That was longer than any job she'd ever had, or would ever have again. As it was, she worried that she hadn't protected her heart nearly as well as she should have. The others had given her a nickname. She was the Ice Queen. It was a reputation that she cultivated with her demeanor and sharp tongue. Avery smiled sadly. In many ways, she was as good at disappearing as Runt.

'We can never stop running. Remember that, honey. If we do, they will find us.'

"I've stayed too long, Momma," Avery murmured. "But they need me now more than ever." She sighed. "I'll finish this mission and re-evaluate what I should do next. I promise."

Avery ignored the tightness in her chest as she leaned forward and shut down the computer system. She rose from her seat and picked up her purse and cell phone. Pressing another number on her slim phone, she lifted it to her ear.

"Have the jet ready to leave for Maine in one hour," she informed the agent.

She turned off the lights and silently exited the office, sealing the door behind her. Minutes later, her driver was waiting outside. He opened the door for her, and she slid inside.

"Where to, Ms. Lennox?" the chauffeur asked.

"My apartment, then the airport, Robert," she murmured.

"You're working late tonight," Robert observed.

"Nothing new," she lightly retorted.

Her eyes briefly met his in the mirror. All she saw was concern. Robert had been with the company Cosmos' parents had started over thirty-five years ago. He had tried retiring, but gave up after a few months and returned to CRI. When Cosmos had decided that Avery should have her own driver, she had argued at first that it wasn't necessary, but then she reluctantly gave in, and now appreciated the fact that she didn't need to worry about the traffic.

Forty minutes later, they were speeding along the expressway to the airport hangar reserved for corporate jets. The black SUV pulled up to the security gate. Robert rolled down the window so the guard could scan Avery's security clearance. Several minutes later, he pulled up next to a luxurious Gulfstream G650. The stewardess, Carol, smiled and reached for her bag as she stepped away from the car.

"Would you care for dinner this evening, Ms. Lennox?" Carol politely asked.

"Yes, please. What's on the menu tonight?" Avery asked, suddenly realizing she was famished.

"There is fresh Salmon with lemon sauce, vegetables, and rice pilaf," Carol replied with a smile. "Anton was delighted when he heard that you would be traveling and thought you might not have had time to eat before we took off."

Avery chuckled. "You both know me too well," she teased, climbing up the steps. "He's right, of course. I haven't had a chance to eat anything."

"I'll let Anton and Rex know you are ready to depart," Carol replied.

"Thank you," Avery murmured, moving to the elegant lounge chair.

She settled in and buckled her seat belt. Looking out the window, she saw Robert wave to Rex, the pilot, as he completed a last minute walk-around. The perks that came with being Head of Security for CRI were nice, but Avery thought of them as tools to do the job—nothing more, nothing less.

"We should be taking off shortly. Is there anything else I can get you for the moment, Ms. Lennox?" Carol politely asked.

Not unless you can deliver a Prime warrior to go with the Salmon and lemon sauce, Avery thought with a wry humor that she hadn't felt in weeks.

Since she didn't think Carol or Cosmos would appreciate her mentioning aliens, she simply shook her head and returned her attention to the window. No, there was nothing Carol could get her for the moment. Cosmos would provide what she needed, and Core had what she wanted: three days of living in a fantasy world.

2

Calais, Maine:

Avery maneuvered the Tesla Roadster around the corner and onto the street that led up to the warehouse where Cosmos Raines lived and worked most of the time. She paused and waited for the doors leading to the underground parking area to automatically open. RITA was tracking her through the car's GPS system.

"Thank you, RITA," Avery chuckled.

"My pleasure, love. I'll meet you inside and make sure you don't have any issues with your trip," RITA cheerfully replied.

"I want to get cleaned up and look over the report before I leave," Avery stated.

"Working after work again, Avery? I know it's hard for you to live for the moment, but if you need someone to talk to, I'm purported to be very discreet," RITA added.

Avery ignored the gentle nudge to open up. Instead, she removed her sunglasses as she pulled into the dark interior of the parking garage. She navigated the Tesla into a parking space with a charging station.

For all of RITA's abilities, she still had her limitations and Avery wasn't looking for a life coach. At first, RITA had been satisfied with the paper trail that Avery had carefully constructed over the years. When RITA had questioned her about something, Avery had taken the AI's inquiry to heart and modified the information until it was iron-clad. No one could know about her past, not even RITA or Cosmos. Unfortunately, RITA's programming had evolved over the years, and once she started interacting with the Prime computer system, she'd been developing a new and even sharper awareness that had Avery on edge.

Yet another reason why it is time to move on, Avery decided, opening the door and sliding out of the car.

She plugged the charger into the car and walked around to the passenger's side, opening the door and grabbing her gear off of the seat before shutting it again with a soft click. The lights of the car briefly flashed, and she heard the locks engage as she walked away.

Minutes later, she was exiting the elevator on the third level. This level used to belong to Jasmine 'Tink' Bell before she moved to Baade, the aliens' home world, to be with her bond mate, J'kar. Avery still thought it was an amusing name for a significant other or spouse, but then, husband and wife probably sounded strange to them.

Since Tink's move to the alien world, Avery had been using her former living space as a temporary command center while working on Avilov and the missing Prime warrior's case. Unfortunately, her presence here had also placed her in contact with Core Ta'Duran. So far, she had managed to keep their relationship distant. They moved around each other like two prize fighters in a ring, sizing each other up. There had been no physical contact—yet. There was little conversation that wasn't terse, and the sexual tension between them was enough to melt the paint off of the walls.

She'd lost count of the number of dreams she'd had of him over the last few months. She always woke up tangled in her Egyptian cotton sheets, aching so badly she was ready to scream. The increasing dreams were making it difficult to concentrate. She would be in the middle of reading a report or in a meeting with her team, only to realize that she had been staring into space, her mind focused on the huge, sexy Prime warrior.

It was time to nip this obsession in the bud. She was the Ice Queen. She could freeze a man's balls off from a hundred paces. Her reaction to Core was simply primal attraction. They were both predators, how could she not want him?

Regardless of her desire, she would not allow her heart to become involved. Love created a vulnerability that could one day be revealed and exploited, no matter how hard a person tried to conceal it. No, once she satisfied her physical desire for Core, she could store the experience away and move on. It wasn't like this was the first time she had been attracted to a man, and it wouldn't be the last.

Perhaps if I keep telling myself this, I'll finally believe what I'm saying, she thought with sardonic amusement.

Avery placed her purse on the small table in the living room and carried her luggage to the guest bedroom at the end of the hallway. One good thing about converting a warehouse into a home—it allowed for ample space in the floor plan. The firm that had designed the layout had done an excellent job. The basement housed the underground parking garage, a generous amount of storage space, and a two-bedroom efficiency. The ground floor was devoted to Cosmos' laboratory. He'd also had a one-bedroom efficiency installed for the times he became engrossed in a project. The second level was Cosmos' private living area. Three huge bedrooms, each with their own bath, a guest bathroom, and an open kitchen/living area made for great entertaining. The third floor was a mirror image of the second. The roof had been reinforced for a helipad, but Cosmos seldom used it. He didn't like to draw attention to himself or the home he considered his favorite.

Avery carried her bag into the bathroom with her. Pulling out fresh clothes and toiletries, she set them out on the counter. Minutes later, she was undressed and standing under the powerful heated spray of the shower with her head bowed and eyes closed.

She groaned in frustration when a vivid image of Core came to her mind and her body tightened and became heated in a way that had nothing to do with the warm water. Opening her eyes, she glared at the shower handles. She reached out and twisted the cold water handle until goosebumps appeared on her skin.

"Well, now I can honestly say I know for a fact that men are not the only ones who have to take a cold shower," she growled with cynical amusement.

She washed her hair and body, hissing as she glided her hand over her sensitive labia and touched her swollen clit. She bowed her head and closed her eyes again. The rueful thought that she should take the edge off of her need flashed through her mind. If she didn't, Core would be in serious trouble.

"Not as much fun, but at the moment it will have to do," Avery grudgingly murmured out loud.

Several minutes later, her soft moan filled the large shower enclosure. A shudder ran through her as some of her tension dissolved. While not completely satisfying, she felt like she had regained a small measure of restraint from the sexual hunger that was driving her crazy.

"So much for outgrowing the need in my youth," she thought with a wry shake of her head.

She reached over and turned off the spray. Opening the door, she grabbed the towel from the hook next to the shower and dried off. Ten minutes later, she was dressed and feeling refreshed. She had blow-dried her shoulder-length, dark brown hair, and it fell in soft, silky waves around her head.

After trying several different styles, she finally settled on pulling her hair into a casual ponytail. The look went with the soft cotton print blouse and blue jeans she had decided to wear. She could count on one hand the number of people who had seen her wearing anything other than her professional attire of a business suit or slacks and silk blouses.

On the vanity were two small, deadly-sharp knives, and a small Ruger LC9 pistol. These were the weapons she carried every day. If she wasn't wearing them, she had them within reach at all times. She carefully strapped on her knives—one on her arm under her long-sleeved blouse and the other just above her ankle-high boot under her jeans. She double-checked the safety of the pistol before sliding it behind her back into the holster at her waist. Then she picked up her soft black leather jacket and slipped it on.

Avery studied her reflection in the mirror. At thirty-two, she was hardly an innocent young woman. She had experienced several short affairs, beginning in her early twenties. The affairs had been calculated, just like her approach with Core.

She had been very careful about choosing her partners. Each man had to meet a certain criteria. They had to be clean—no drugs, no wife or girlfriend, no alcohol abuse, and very discreet.

She didn't care about their monetary worth. After all, their relationship was not about fostering an emotional connection. She never chose men who lived in the same city and never invited them to her residence. She also never told them her real name.

Since her employment with CRI, she had refrained from having a relationship with anyone. The first year had been the most difficult. Luckily, there were enough stores to find the items that she wanted in Houston to take the edge off when it became necessary.

She had not planned on staying with CRI so long. A chance encounter with Cosmos had led to her employment. Her respect for him had made her stay. She believed in what he was doing for the world. Cosmos Raines was absolutely brilliant. His inventions were unbelievably advanced, as evidenced by RITA. The fact that his inventions were now integrated with alien technology only made them more impressive.

Which didn't change the fact that it had been a *long* time since Avery had been with someone. There wasn't really a dilemma to agonize over, Avery just felt… nervous, she supposed. This felt big, and not just because she'd be mixing business with pleasure. She and Core would amicably part ways after their three days of incredible sex, and Core wouldn't need to return to Earth. If he did, it wasn't necessary for them to be in close contact again since his cousin had been located. Even if Core decided to visit Earth again—which he shouldn't need to do—she could always find work at another of CRI's facilities around the world. Or she could find another job.

Who was she kidding? CRI was the perfect place for her. There was no way she could leave. The work, the people, and the cause was what she'd been programmed from birth to live for.

Besides, she had been doing a lot of thinking since the revelation of the Gateway and life on other worlds. It was time to discuss a few changes with Cosmos. Now that aliens were part of the security equation, and especially since Cosmos' wife, Terra, was one, Avery felt it was doubly important to re-evaluate and revise CRI's security plans.

Amelia, aka the Runt, was part of the team now, and she could take over threat containment on the alien side of things, while Avery took on a more active role in bringing down those responsible for the criminal activities that were too hot for governments even to admit were happening.

Taking in a deep breath, Avery looked into the vanity mirror, and smoothed a tendril of hair that had escaped from her hair tie. The memory of her mother doing the same thing flashed through her mind followed by a shaft of remorse. She'd inherited her mother's features and her father's coloring. She'd also been taught their espionage skills. What she would not accept was that she could have inherited their weakness—falling in love.

If Core refused to accept her terms, if he wanted a long-term relationship—well, that would be difficult under the best of circumstances. Even an uncomplicated relationship lasting a few weeks or months would be almost impossible considering they literally lived on different worlds.

No, if he didn't accept her terms, she would have to return to Earth unsatisfied and move on. She firmly believed that some people had to have the white picket fence and lifelong love, and some people were destined for more difficult, but more fulfilling lives. Avery's destiny was to fight for those who couldn't.

There were others who felt the same way—Tansy Bell was one of them. But, Tansy—like Avery's parents—had made the mistake of falling in love. When that happened, priorities changed. Unfortunately, those who perpetuated evil didn't have the same weaknesses. They continue to wreak havoc on the world—leaving grief and destruction behind.

Avery raised an eyebrow at her reflection and wryly smiled. She looked cool and confident—two aspects of her demeanor that had become her trademark over the years. Both would work in her favor—they always had before. Unfortunately, on the inside she was feeling incredibly hot and surprisingly unsure about a number of things. Everything that she'd felt certain she knew about what she wanted was suddenly not as clear as she'd thought it was.

It was time to make a choice and follow through. She would have to make sure that Core accepted her terms. If not, she wasn't sure there were enough batteries in the world to handle her battery-operated boyfriend.

"Okay, now you're just being melodramatic. You're never melodramatic, Avery. What kind of guy, especially one who is attracted to you, would turn down three full days of unadulterated, mindless sex with no strings attached?" she asked her reflection.

She chuckled when she saw the expression on her face. With a shake of her head, she grinned and turned away from the mirror. She had her answer—not a damn one that she knew of!

Humming under her breath, she returned to the living room where she had placed her purse. She reached out and paused, impulsively deciding that she would leave it. She highly doubted that she would need her identification on Baade. Hell, she was almost tempted to leave her small bag of clothes. She was hoping that she wouldn't need them either—but she also had a few weapons in the bag that she carried everywhere. She unzipped the bag and looked at the two guns lying on top of her clothing. One had belonged to her father; the other had belonged to her mother. They had left them at home the day they were murdered, and Avery had later retrieved them from their hiding place along with other weapons, cash, and fake identities. She slid the zipper closed without removing the weapons.

"Oh, Avery, you have it bad, girl," she muttered.

For a moment, she could hear her father's voice in her head. She closed her eyes and pictured him and her mother standing in front of her. The first time she had heard the rhyme, she was barely old enough to walk. She could still hear her mother chiding her father for teaching her to sing the words like a song. She would always remember the quiet intensity in her father's voice as he encouraged her to sing along with him.

'Listen, Avery, to your head, otherwise you'll end up dead,' her father had told her over and over.

She quietly recited the rhyme her father had taught her as a wave of melancholy swept through her. She picked up the small bag and slipped the strap over her shoulder. Straightening her shoulders, she pushed the memories away and refocused on her current mission: Core Ta'Duran.

"RITA, do you have Core Ta'Duran's position?" she inquired.

"Yes, love. My sister was rather delighted that you are coming to visit. She said that Core returned to check on his clan and inform his mother that Merrick is out of danger and resting. He really is such a considerate man," RITA hinted.

Avery snorted. "Yes, Matchmaker RITA, he's perfect. Please just program the coordinates for me. I'll handle the rest," she retorted.

"Yes, Avery," RITA replied, her voice tinged with disappointment.

"Thank you, RITA," Avery murmured in a softer tone.

Avery stepped into the elevator and pressed her hand to the control screen. A thin green light scanned her palm. RITA had already programmed the level for her. The elevator would go to the first floor, but only with security clearance would the rear door open into the lab. She waited as the elevator door opened.

A set of titanium bars parted and an array of laser sensors shut off. With a grimace, she decided she might have gone a little overboard with the increased security around the portal as she took five steps forward and paused on the weighted mat. The secondary security system activated. She was now trapped between the sealed elevator and the twelve-inch-thick, clear, bullet-and-bomb-proof entryway into the lab.

Lifting her arms, she waited as a full body scan along with facial recognition was completed. Even though RITA had verified her presence, Avery had been paranoid that RITA could be compromised.

"Can I open the doors now?" RITA's dry voice asked.

"Yes, please. You know, this is to protect you as much as Cosmos, Terra, and the Prime home world," Avery informed the computer system as the doors parted.

She jumped when RITA's corporeal form suddenly appeared in front of her after she stepped through the doors. Her hand fluttered up to her chest, and she glared at the gorgeous redhead in a glittering red evening gown.

"FRED and I have made a few improvements of our own, love. It is very unlikely that anyone—here or on Baade—could get through our defenses," RITA reassured her.

Avery looked RITA up and down with a frown. "Why are you wearing an evening gown?" she asked in confusion.

"It is date night. FRED is taking me to a performance in New York. You aren't the only one who needs a little fun, Avery," RITA drawled in a mischievous tone.

The AI's green eyes danced with delight. Her expression wouldn't have been quite so intimidating if RITA's eyes hadn't been glowing with brilliant little dots of code running through her irises. Avery shook her head.

"I don't want to know any of the details," Avery stated with a lift of her hand. "At least not until I get back. Then I want to know every delicious morsel," she added.

RITA's delighted laugh sounded chillingly real. "Only if you do a little sharing yourself," she teased.

Avery stepped through RITA and continued down the stairs to the main section of the laboratory where Cosmos had left the portal device for her. There were a lot of things in this world that Avery didn't talk about, and her sex life was one of them.

"Have fun, RITA. I'll return in three days," Avery replied, snatching up the small cylinder.

"You, too, Avery," RITA quietly replied, watching as Avery activated the device.

Avery breathed deeply when a shimmering doorway appeared in front of her. On the other side, she could see rich wood, a huge bed, a lush forest, and a beaming RITA2. Avery decided it had been a smart decision to wear jeans instead of her normal pantsuit and heels. Lifting her chin in determination, she released the breath she had been holding and stepped through the portal—to the alien world.

3

Prime Home World of Baade:
Forest of the Eastern Clan

Core strode through the village toward the modest home he was constructing in a large tree on the outskirts. Since Merrick's disappearance, Core had split his time between Baade and Earth, fulfilling his responsibilities as temporary leader of the Eastern Mountain Clan and searching for his cousin and best friend.

He had learned a lot over the past six months. First, that leading a large clan of primarily men was not an easy task. Each of them longed for a bond mate. The few women in the village were either too young —like his sister—or had already found their mates.

Tempers flared easily among them. Core rotated his stiff shoulders, and winced. He'd relieved some of the strain through sparring, and this morning a first-year warrior from the village had struck a good blow to Core's shoulder when thoughts of Avery had diminished his focus. He couldn't seem to do anything without thinking of her, and the others were not much better. Tension among the men had grown since they learned that there was a planet where a bond mate could be found. He swore that every single one of them had a crush on the Bell women—especially Tilly!

Her weekly Chick-flick movies had become a must-see. She was doing a Romantic Comedy, or RC, marathon this weekend. For once, Core was glad that he had the entire village to himself.

"Core, where are you going?" a young voice called out from behind him.

Core slowed to a stop and closed his eyes. A soft groan escaped him. He'd almost made it without being seen. With a sigh of resignation, he slowly turned to face his excited sister, Nadine.

"I have work to do," he answered.

Nadine scowled at him and placed her hands on her hips. "You are always working! Mother said you should have balance. We are going to Lady Tilly's RC Festival. Won't you please come?" Nadine begged.

Core shook his head. "Not this time. I want to work on my new home," he gently replied.

"I really want you to come," she begged.

Nadine's face fell. It was hard to resist the disappointed pout on her lips. He almost gave in until he saw the glimmer of amusement in her eyes. He flashed her a suspicious look.

"What are you up to?" he asked.

Nadine's expression changed, and she grinned at him. "Did you forget that you promised that I could drive the glider?" she asked.

He groaned, and ran his hand over his face. Yes, he had forgotten. Lately, he had been forgetting a lot. Between Merrick's abduction and rescue, dealing with the clan's troubles, and being haunted by Avery. He was lucky he remembered to do the simple things in life like eat and sleep.

His gaze softened when he looked up and saw his mother. She had taken over organizing and running things here while he and Merrick were gone. She smiled at him in understanding.

"I can show her, Core. The village will be empty this weekend. Why don't you enjoy the peace and quiet?" Nadu offered.

"Make sure that she keeps it in low gear. Tink and Tilly modified my glider while I was at the palace," he warned.

Nadu laughed and shook her head. "We'll take mine," she replied.

"But, Nadu, I wanted to go fast!" Nadine complained.

Nadu reined in her smile with some difficulty and put on her stern face, though her eyes were dancing with merriment. "You can go faster once you know how to control the glider. Now come or we will miss the previews," she ordered.

"Thank you," he called out behind his mother.

"Thank me by bringing home a bond mate so I can have another daughter," Nadu teasingly called over her shoulder.

Core dryly chuckled before he tiredly ran both hands over his face. He would love to give his mother a new daughter to dote on. He even knew exactly who the woman would be!

The problem was convincing the hard-headed human female. For months now, he had been trying to get close to Avery. Every time he got within a few feet of her, she would suddenly find a way to elude him.

Core watched as Nadine excitedly climbed into the older model four-seater glider. He really needed to purchase a new one for his mother. He winced when he saw the glider rock from side to side as it lifted off the ground.

He stood there until he could no longer see the glider. It took him several more minutes to realize that the forest was unusually quiet. Gone were the sounds of laughter and the chatter of people going about their daily chores. He looked around the deserted village, feeling both a sense of pride and a touch of panic.

"Is this what my life will be like? Quiet, lonely—empty," he murmured despondently.

He slowly turned and resumed walking back toward his construction, his thoughts inevitably returning to Avery.

When he reached the path that led to his home, he paused and studied his work in progress. He had picked a tall tree near the river. His home had four levels at the moment. The lower level consisted of a deck that looked out over the river. A winding walkway ramp led to the next level, which held the living area, kitchen, two bathing units, a guest bedroom, den, library, and sun deck. The inner staircase wound around the tree to the upper level that consisted of four bedrooms with individual bathing units—still under construction—and a common living area with a smaller deck that overlooked the river on one side and the village on the other. The staircase continued up to the topmost level which contained the master bedroom. He'd been thinking of Avery when he added that level. The room was open, airy, and it was made for enjoying the beauty of the surrounding forest.

The sitting room on that level's hexagonal deck overlooked a waterfall cascading into the river below. Wild, exotic birds in a variety of colors rested on the deck railing. Their songs mixed with the sound of the wind through the trees and the splash and gurgle of the water below.

A large bathing unit wrapped around the trunk of the tree. He had used the minimum amount of solid walls, preferring to leave the view as unobstructed as possible. Clear double-pane glass would automatically rise and protect the room from the rain or shield them from the sun if they wished.

Doors led out onto the tree's thick branches and to smaller covered areas meant for lounging. He was also constructing bridges from his home to the village so there would be no need to descend to the ground below.

Each tree lived thousands of years. He had picked one that was nearly three hundred years old and still growing. Each tree trunk was hollow, which made an inner lift system possible, and certain branches had large, naturally occurring openings, which he could use to access each level of the home.

His clan carefully monitored the trees for signs of disease, and the bark contained a natural insect repellent. There were only two things from which his people's trees died: old age and intentional destruction.

It was against the law of his clan to purposely damage any of their trees, because it only made sense to preserve what gave them shelter. The fruit from the trees also gave them food and a source of income.

The highly sought after and very nutritious palm-sized fruit varied from tree to tree. Some produced a nut while others produced a sweet, meaty fruit. The decaying fallen leaves from these trees also contributed to the fertile soil, allowing the Eastern Mountain Clan to grow staples that their replicators had a difficult time reproducing.

It took him a moment to realize he was trying to see his home and village from a different perspective. He was imagining what Avery would see when—if—she ever saw it. Would she think them primitive? Her city had hard streets and buildings everywhere. Bright lights lit up the night sky and outshone the stars.

His people had learned to live with the world around them, and tried not to change it too drastically. He thought it was a harmonious and logical way to live, but would Avery feel the same? He had never seen her looking anything but cool, calm, and elegantly dressed... and of course she would be armed to the teeth. Just like that, Core was vividly imagining removing the weapons she kept hidden under her clothes. Her eyes would be filled with passion as he unwound her hair from its neat twist.

He sighed and shook his head. *Before I can do any of that, I need to get close enough to touch her—not to mention the part where I ask for her permission. I don't want to end up with a knife in my gut or a hole in my head,* he thought with sardonic amusement.

Realizing that he'd been standing lost in thought for long enough, he strode down the path to his home. He needed another cold shower.

He swept his gaze through the woods to the river, and grinned as an idea formed in his mind. It had been a long time since he'd gone swimming in the basin below the waterfall. Hot springs fed into it. He could soak his sore muscles before cooling off.

He detoured, and several minutes later, he was near the hot springs. The water flowed over the basin's edge and gushed downstream. A cool mist from the surrounding waterfalls provided a refreshing contrast to the heat. This area was a favorite among warriors and families alike. It was strange to have it all to himself.

"I may have to ask Tilly to do more programs," he mused as he removed his belt.

Within minutes, he was undressed and stepping into the hot spring. He groaned as the warm water covered his legs, then he sank down into the healing depths, letting the heat pull the soreness out of his neck and shoulders.

"Now, if only Avery were here," he murmured, leaning his head back against the basin's edge and closing his eyes.

..*

"Are you sure this is it?" Avery asked, looking around the beautiful interior.

"Of course, honey. I'm never wrong; just ask DAR," RITA2 brightly replied.

"Like I would ever admit that you could make a miscalculation, my dear," DAR dryly remarked, suddenly appearing.

Avery gave herself ten points for not jumping when the holographic image changed and became more corporeal. These AI systems were advancing so rapidly that she was wondering if mankind's existence was on the threshold of being replaced.

RITA2 was almost an exact replica of Cosmos and Tilly's creation back on Earth. So much so that Avery had to search hard to find the barely discernable difference and reassure herself that she was indeed talking to a completely different system. One thing the two AIs definitely had in common was that sweet but mischievous smile that made the hairs on the back of Avery's neck stand up.

"This is Core's home," RITA2 replied, walking around the room with a curious expression.

"And you just happened to open the portal into his bedroom," Avery observed.

RITA2 turned and looked at her with an innocent expression. "Well, it is where you were hoping to spend the next three days, wasn't it?" the curvy AI inquired.

"Thank you, I think I can take it from here," she said, pocketing the portable gateway device.

"Avery… perhaps you should—" RITA2 started to say. She sighed when Avery shot her a warning look.

"I've got this," Avery quietly interjected.

RITA2 looked up at DAR when he silently wrapped his arm around her waist. Avery couldn't believe that a computer program had the ability to make her feel a tinge of guilt. She must be getting soft.

"The gateway device is programmed to return you to the location you departed from," RITA2 instructed.

"Thank you," Avery replied.

"Oh, and before we leave I should tell you that you and Core are alone. Tilly is putting on a wonderful romantic comedy film festival if you get bored," she chuckled before fading.

Avery released a short laugh. Only Tilly Bell would think of having a romance film festival on an alien world filled with horny men and not enough women. Now that she was alone, Avery looked around the room again.

The room was masculine, but nothing seemed too overwhelmingly 'Man Cave'. She walked across the room and placed her bag on a chair before stepping close to the low wall that ran the length of the room. Her lips parted in amazement. The house was situated high in a tree.

A startled gasp escaped her when a bright purple bird, at least she thought it was a bird, landed outside the window. The creature had wings and flew like a bird, but it also had four legs. The bird had a bright yellow crest that fluttered up and down when he bobbed his head.

"Don't mess with me. I like to eat chicken," she warned with wry amusement when the bird tilted his head and looked at her.

The bird emitted several deep-throated notes and Avery chuckled as it took off. She leaned forward to watch it fly through the branches, then gasped again and froze, amazed at the sight beyond the bird. She would have missed the movement if she hadn't been following the flight pattern of the bird.

A soft, approving whistle slipped from her lips. Core was climbing out of a small, dark blue pool of steaming water. He stood and stretched before rolling his shoulders. Avery thoroughly appreciated every movement. Her imagination had *not* done justice to Core's chiseled physique.

"I swear the man has muscles on top of muscles," she admired.

She narrowed her eyes and a thoughtful look came into them. Her gaze followed his graceful movements when he climbed onto a rock before he dove into the larger pool of water. Turning on her heel, she retraced her steps to her bag. Unzipping it, Avery dug to the bottom and pulled out a sarong that she had picked up in Indonesia.

She stripped out of her clothing, exchanging her short boots for a pair of slip on sandals. Her hand wavered as she reached for her gun and two knives, and paused. She decided to compromise—she kept on the knife strapped to her ankle before wrapping the sarong around her and tucking the end to keep it secure. She placed the other two weapons back into her bag.

Peering out the window, she saw Core casually swim across the wide pool. She strode to the center of the room, and placed her hand on the panel near a door. She was relieved when it opened to reveal a lift. Stepping inside, she looked around. There was no interior panel that she could see.

"Down," she instructed.

"Welcome, Avery. Which level would you like?" RITA2's voice asked.

"Are you serious? You've taken over their home computer system?" Avery asked in disbelief.

"Of course! How else can I assist you if you need help while you're here?" RITA2 cheerfully replied.

Avery shook her head. "I want to get to the ground so I can go to the waterfall," she stated.

"Very well; Forest Floor," RITA2 said.

"You can't see what happens on each level, can you?" Avery asked, suddenly wondering if this was such a good idea after all.

"Of course not! I'm not programmed that way," RITA2 retorted in an indignant tone. "Forest Floor. If you go to the right, there is a path that will lead you directly to the falls."

Avery stepped out of the lift, amazed at the spacious, clear tubular elevator hidden inside the tree. Excitement filled her. The realization that she was on an alien world and about to have the hottest affair of her life was finally sinking in. She followed the path through the forest and along the river, secure in the knowledge that she would not deviate from her plan. Three days was the limit. Any longer, and she would be tempted to push for one more day and then another one until the days became weeks and the weeks became months and her heart became inextricably entangled.

Her mother said that was what had happened with Avery's father. They'd met on opposing missions, were drawn to each other, and one thing had led to the next. Avery had later come to the conclusion that her parents had been selfish and greedy. They had wanted something that they knew was impossible and had tried to have it all.

If they had loved each other and lived with the risks, that would have been fine, but they'd had her, and their desire to have a life filled with true happiness in a dark and dangerous world had led to their deaths, had made her an orphan, had almost killed her, and it had caused the death of another innocent child.

She would not make the same mistake. Three days was as much as she knew deep in her heart that she could give Core. If she stayed any longer, she would begin to think selfishly.

As far as greed went, Avery knew she didn't have to worry. Any desire to take more than she should have had left her when she lay covered in blood that day on the soccer field.

Avery pushed the morbid thoughts away. These were her three days. There would be no thinking of the past or what the future would hold.

She took a deep breath of the clean, fresh air. All around her were beautiful plants, colorful birds singing in harmony, and the soothing sound of flowing water. She paused at the edge of the forest near the hot springs where Core had first emerged, searching the pool for him.

She parted her lips on a sigh when he climbed up onto a set of rocks on the far side, and she was greeted by the view of his very firm and muscular buttocks. She barely had time to admire them before he turned around and gave her a frontal view that she knew would be forever burned into her mind.

Her gaze caressed him from his short hair to his strong jaw, over his broad shoulders and flat stomach, lingering there before following the patch of dark hair to his groin.

"Sweet alien encounters, but that man is.... Please let him agree to the three days! Please!" Avery muttered under her breath.

As he dove back into the pool, she stepped out of the forest, walked across the sandy ground, and dropped her sarong on top of his pile of clothing. She pulled the rubber band from her hair and dropped it on top as well, then walked to the edge of the crystal clear water and began to wade into its warmth. Once she was deep enough, she dove forward and began to swim toward him.

4

Core turned on his back and floated. His body was relaxed, even if his mind refused to calm. He stared up at the sky, watching the clouds as they passed by, and following an occasional bird as it swooped from one tree to another on the other side of the river.

He moved his arms and legs back and forth to keep his body from sinking while his mind swirled with an endless list of arguments to get Avery to accept their destiny. His latest thought was that he could try kidnapping her.

And end up dead. Still, it might be worth the risk if I can at least touch her just once before I die, he mused.

No, kidnapping was out. He'd learned a very painful lesson when it came to kidnapping human women: they fight back and they don't do it fairly. When he and his cousin, Merrick, had impulsively decided to kidnap Hannah Bell to learn more about her species and where they had come from, she had knocked him out and escaped out into the forest. His heart still pounded every time he remembered her running through the trees. His groin still hurt every time he thought about how it had felt when her knee had rammed into it.

He had to find some way to convince Avery. All he needed was to touch her once. If the mark of the mating ritual appeared—and he felt sure it would—there would be no denying that they were meant to be together.

He was so lost in thought that the sudden splash of water over his face startled him. He whirled around, briefly submerging, then kicking upward. He broke the surface and wildly looked around.

The sound of a husky laugh drew his attention. His eyes widened when he looked into the vivid blue eyes of the woman he had been daydreaming about.

"You know, for a Prime warrior who is supposed to be so big and bad, you really aren't that difficult to sneak up on," she teased with a mocking smile.

Fire licked through Core's veins. His eyes glittered in response to the challenge in her eyes. He slowly swam toward her, and she didn't move away.

"Why are you here?" he demanded, pausing less than a foot from her.

They both treaded water, maintaining the distance between them as they moved in a graceful circle. Her expression was determined. A glimmer of suspicion coursed through him. She was not here to admit that they belonged together. He could still see the unmistakable wall of reserve in her eyes.

"I have a proposition," she announced.

A frown of confusion creased his brow. "A proposition? What type of proposition?" he warily asked.

"Three days—no strings, no demands, no expectations beyond those three days of mindless sex and each other's company," she calmly replied.

A fierce, swift denial rose to his lips. He stopped the words before they were uttered, replaying her words in his mind. His focus returned to the words 'mindless sex.'

"And if I refuse this proposition?" he asked.

She shrugged her shoulders and looked away. "If that is what you want," she replied.

Before he could say anything else, she slipped beneath the water.

He looked around him, trying to find her, then turned when he heard her draw in a breath. She was several yards from him.

As Core watched as Avery cut through the water with strong strokes, it suddenly dawned on him that she thought he had rebuffed her. He kicked out with powerful strokes of his own, and reached the shallow edge of the water just as she was wading onto the sandy beach.

He stood up in the waist-deep water as she paused to pick up a colorful piece of cloth from the top of his pile of clothing. Her lithe body was extremely distracting. He noted her slender shoulders, long waist, and smooth buttocks before taking in her long legs. He frowned when his gaze reached her ankles.

"Are you wearing a blade?" he asked, wading out of the water.

She looked over her shoulder at him as she tied the fabric around herself. There was just a slight curve to her lips. His body immediately hardened when she gazed at him with an appreciative expression, pausing on his groin. He might have maintained a portion of his dignity if she hadn't licked her lips. A soft groan slipped from him as his cock responded to her tease. Damn that recording of Tink telling J'kar's crew about oral sex! Now he wanted to know if one of the things J'kar's mate had shared was true!

"I did not say that I would not accept your proposition. I merely asked what would happen if I did not. What if I wanted to add some conditions?" he demanded.

She turned to face him. "What kind of conditions?" she asked.

He stopped a foot away from her. "Touch my hand," he instructed.

Core held his hand out to her, palm up.

She lifted one delicate eyebrow before she reached out. Her hand hovered above his for a moment before she pressed her palm to his. A startled hiss escaped her, and she jerked her hand back with a scowl.

"Static electricity," she muttered, clenching her hand and holding it against her chest.

He looked down at his own hand. A sense of awe swept through him when he saw the intricate patterns forming in the center of his palm. He looked up at her and shook his head.

"No, not static electricity," he contradicted with a wry grin. "This is something far more powerful.

He turned his palm toward her so she could see the mark. "I knew we were destined to be together the moment I saw you," he quietly said.

She looked at his palm and frowned, then slowly uncurled her fingers and stared at her own hand. Her jaw tightened, and her lips pursed together.

He waited for her to respond.

"This was a mistake," she finally replied, looking up at him.

He watched in stunned disbelief when she turned and started walking away. Bending, he grabbed his trousers and pulled them on before gathering the rest of his clothing and his boots. It didn't take him long to catch up with her.

"That is all you have to say? That our bond is a mistake?" he demanded.

"There is no bond," she retorted, pausing briefly to slip into her shoe.

Core skidded to a stop. He reached out and wrapped the hand holding his clothing around her waist to keep from knocking her over. She turned her head and glared at him. He couldn't stop the crooked grin that curved his lips.

"You need to call out a warning before you stop," he teased, trying to lighten the moment.

She released an inelegant snort and finished slipping on her other sandal. "You should not follow so closely behind me," she snapped.

He released her when she pulled away. With a soft curse, he bent over and picked up the vest that he had dropped, then strode after her, his narrowed eyes focused on her stiff back. The sheer wrap did little to cover her. He could clearly see every detail of her delectable body underneath.

"What are you planning to do?" he asked when he realized that she was heading straight for his home.

She glanced over her shoulder at him before she refocused on where she was heading. Her expression was regretful… and haunted.

His stomach tightened in response. She shook her head and stepped onto the path that led to the front of his home.

He reached out and grasped her arm, uncaring that the items in his hands fell to the ground again. This time he used both hands to gently turn her around so she was forced to look at him. She tilted her head and stared up into his eyes.

"I'm going to gather my clothes, get dressed, and return to my world," she quietly stated.

"What about us?" he demanded with a frown. "You cannot ignore that we are bond mates, Avery. The mating mark would not have formed if we weren't."

"I don't believe in mating marks, bond mates, or the boogeyman. I don't do bonding. I came for sex—three mindless days of anything-goes-before-we-go our-own-way sex. Obviously that isn't something you are interested in. It was worth a try," she said.

He tightened his grip on her arms when she tried to turn away, realizing that she meant what she was saying. She had no idea that their being apart would be impossible from now on. There was no going back now that they had been matched. She would feel the intense need to be near him as much as he would. He had to make her understand.

"Avery…" he began.

"Let me go, Core. This was a mistake. I should have listened to my gut," she ordered, stiffly pulling out of his arms and turning away.

"I agree to your proposition," he said.

She froze before slowly turning to look at him again with a suspicious expression. "You agree?" she repeated.

He gave a sharp nod of his head. "Yes, three days of mindless sex," he quietly said.

The look of suspicion slowly melted from her eyes and a surprisingly excited smile lit up her features. Her gaze ran down his body. His cock immediately reacted to the hungry look in her eyes.

"Starting now," she murmured, walking toward him.

Core groaned when she pulled off the strip of material from her body and let it fall to the ground. He immediately reached for her breasts. This was so different from everything he had learned. Females were supposed to be indifferent, accepting of a male, but not aggressive, and not passionate until she had been driven mindless by the bite and her lover's skill. This was more like what Tink and Tilly had talked about.

It was definitely much more exciting this way. Core slid his hands along the sides of her breasts before he held them in his palms. They fit perfectly. He brushed his thumbs across her swollen nipples. She softly moaned and stepped closer to him.

"It's a good thing everyone loves Tilly's romantic weekends, otherwise this could be a little hard to explain," she chuckled, sliding her hands down his chest to his pants. "You are way overdressed."

"Sweet Goddess! How can a warrior ever be this honored?" Core hissed when she released his trousers and wrapped her hand around his engorged cock. He tightened his hold on her breasts.

He had discreetly watched the affection the Bell women bestowed upon their Prime mates, especially their curious habit of pressing their lips together in what they called a kiss. Now, he was experiencing the unimaginable rush of pleasure when Avery leaned forward and pressed her lips to his.

He parted his lips in surprise when she ran her tongue along his lower lip. She immediately slipped her tongue inside his mouth, deepening the kiss as she stroked him with one hand and wrapped the other firmly around his neck.

He rocked his hips in rhythm with her movements. As the haze of desire and pulsing need thundered through his body, he impatiently kicked off his trousers. He slid one arm around Avery's back, the other behind her knees, and picked her up.

She leaned her head back against his shoulder and wickedly smiled up at him. His silver-colored eyes flashed with suppressed emotion. His body was taut with the need to join with her.

"Please note that I like my sex hot and often," she murmured, pressing open-mouthed kisses to his neck.

"Sweet Goddess, you'll have me coming before I reach the lift," he growled.

She leaned back and looked at him with a raised eyebrow. "Have you ever made love in a lift before?" she inquired.

He paused in front of the entrance to his home and looked down at her. His body was demanding that he take her, yet his mind wanted to treat her with the respect that she deserved. The doubt raging through his mind disappeared when she reached up and bit his neck.

"How often do you want to make love?" he demanded in a strangled tone.

"That is a loaded question," she teased. "I think it depends on how fast you can reload."

It took a second for her double meaning to sink in. This was a side of Avery that he'd never expected. The Ice Queen hid a woman that captured his imagination with her fiery passion.

"I hope you can keep up," he bit back with a challenging gleam in his eyes.

"Open the door and find out," she dared.

Core shifted her in his arms and pressed his palm against the panel next to the door. He stepped inside the moment it opened. Before the doors closed, he was pressing her up against the wall of the lift.

5

Avery threaded her fingers through Core's hair as he lowered her feet to the ground and pressed her up against the wall. She pulled his head toward her, hungrily capturing his mouth in a deep, desperate, passion-filled kiss.

She explored his mouth with the same attention to detail that she did everything in her life. She noted his sharp teeth, his firm lips, and the pure pleasure of tasting him. She pulled back when her tongue swept along his teeth again. A shiver ran through her when the tip touched his canine. It was much longer than it had been before.

She heard Core release a shuddering moan when she ran her tongue along his elongated tooth. Curious, she touched the other one. It was elongated as well. It appeared that there were some things she needed to learn about her alien soon-to-be lover. There was nothing in the database about the Prime's sexual habits—only their fighting capabilities.

Her breath caught when he suddenly lifted her by the waist. She wrapped her arms around his neck and her long legs around his hips. He gripped her thighs, holding her in place before he slowly relaxed his grip. She felt his cock press against her heated entrance. The thick bulbous head pushed through her wet folds and slowly penetrated her.

Avery tightly held him as her body adjusted to his large shaft. Their breath mixed as they joined. For a brief moment the thought that Core wasn't wearing any protection swept through her mind before she pushed it away. It didn't matter. She couldn't get pregnant, and according to the information she had obtained from RITA's database on Prime Warriors, they did not have sexually transmitted diseases like humans did—probably due to the limited number of available women.

Avery let go of all rational thought after that and focused on the overload of sensations swamping her body. A soft hiss escaped her as she relaxed around his cock. She reluctantly broke their kiss so she could watch his face. A tender smile curved her lips when she saw his intense expression and closed eyes.

With one arm still looped around his neck, she reached up with her right hand and caressed his cheek. He slowly opened his eyes and stared back at her with twin silver flames burning in his eyes. That look was so powerful it felt like her heart actually skipped a beat.

"Core…" she murmured, pressing a kiss to the corner of his mouth.

"You have no idea how long I have dreamed of this moment, Avery," he said in a harsh voice. "There have been so many nights when I dreamed that I was holding you in my arms but woke with them empty."

She leaned her head back, tightened her thighs, and lifted her body just enough to feel his long shaft slide along her slick channel. A shudder ran through him at her deliberate tease of his senses. The flames grew in his eyes as she lowered herself back down.

"I'm here now. That's all that matters," she said, capturing his lips again.

He kissed her back with a possessiveness that turned her on, and rocked his hips in a fast rhythmic cadence that heated her blood. When he released her lips, she tilted her head back against the side of the lift. He thrust faster, his fingers curling into the flesh of her thighs.

She clung to his shoulders, trying to keep from completely melting. She felt his hot breath against her neck and turned her head slightly to give him better access.

"Oh, yes. Oh, baby, yes, just like that," she breathlessly murmured.

Her muscles tightened, and she could feel the tingling beginning of an orgasm. The fact that her sensitive nipples were brushing against his chest as he moved helped her arousal peak.

Avery dug her heels into Core's buttocks as she climaxed. His savage snarl echoed in the lift a second before she felt a sharp prick of pain on her neck followed by a wave of heated pleasure.

Her passionate cry drove him crazy. His grip on her thighs tightened, and he lifted her up enough to pin her firmly between the wall and his body—her grip on his shoulders holding her upright as he took her with an intensity that left her gasping.

Her muscles clamped down on him as she came hard. She closed her eyes as wave after wave of pleasure scorched her. She trembled and curled her fingers into his flesh, leaving the imprint of her sharp nails.

Avery swore she could feel every succulent inch of his cock as he moved within her swollen sheath. She focused and her inner muscles squeezed him harder until she swore it felt like they would never be separated again. His low, guttural groan was muffled against her shoulder as he found his release.

He slid one arm under her buttocks while his other wrapped around her back, and leaned forward, his teeth still buried in the curve of her neck. They stood like that for several minutes before he carefully released his grip on her neck and ran his tongue over the marks to speed up the healing process. She leaned her forehead against his shoulder. She could still feel his cock pulsing inside her.

"You do realize that you never started the lift, and we are still on the ground," she said with a chuckle.

"That will give you time to be ready for the next round. You've given me the pleasure of your company and mindless sex for just three days, and I plan to take advantage of every second. I will be recharged by the time we get to our bedroom. You'd better be ready," he promised.

Avery lifted her head and looked at him with wide, astonished eyes. He was serious. The grin on her face widened.

"Well, damn. I do believe this is going to be one hell of a vacation after all," she muttered before capturing his lips again.

Core kept looking at the faint mark on Avery's neck where he had bitten her. She softly hummed under her breath as she sliced some of the bread his mother had baked for him the day before. Her hair was still damp from the shower they had taken a short while ago.

He still couldn't believe that she was here. The past three hours had been incredible. His body pleasantly throbbed, and for now he was content just looking at her. One pale shoulder was exposed where her sleeve had slid down. Her shirt stopped at mid-thigh, revealing her long, slender legs. He itched to remove the soft, oversized shirt from her body.

"You'll never finish cutting up that fruit if you don't stop looking at me," she teased.

He grinned. "I am afraid to take my eyes off of you in case you disappear," he admitted.

She walked over to him and picked up a piece of fruit. The expression in his eyes darkened when she took a bite, then lifted the other half to his lips. His mouth instinctively opened, and he leaned forward, taking the juicy offering from her fingers before he wrapped his fingers around her wrist. He kept his gaze focused on her face as he drew her fingers to his lips. In a slow, deliberately seductive move, he ran his tongue along her fingers, licking the sweet juice from them.

Her gaze followed the movement of his tongue. He could sense her body's reaction, and the evidence of his arousal was clearly visible in the lightweight trousers he had slipped on after their shower.

"Damn you! You are making me want to forget about eating everything but you," she groaned.

He chuckled. "We were taught as young men that it would take great stimulation to arouse our bond mate, that only the chemical in our bite and the connection between us could create a satisfying joining. I have only to look at you and I am on fire," he confessed, pressing her fingers against his lips as he spoke.

Her eyes danced with wicked amusement as she skimmed her other hand down his chest and across his flat stomach. His hips jerked forward when she slipped her fingers beneath the waistband of his pants to grasp his cock.

"Well, I think it is time for a new lesson. You know, I'm really not that hungry—for food," she murmured.

A shuddering breath escaped him when she pulled her fingers free. He wanted to protest when she released his cock, but the words died when she gripped the top of his pants, pulled them down, and knelt in front of him. His eyes widened when she gripped his cock again—and slowly wrapped her lips around it.

"Ja tasn meszk talkok!" I must be dreaming, he hissed as his body was engulfed in pleasure.

He reached behind him and gripped the counter, curling his fingers around the edge as he watched her head move back and forth. He was mesmerized by the hot warmth of her mouth surrounding him, the way she was teasing him with her tongue, and the tight grip of her fingers pumping his engorged shaft.

Core gulped when she gazed up at him with a knowing look. He trembled as he tried to hold onto his control. He might have held on a little longer if she hadn't reached down between her legs and began to pleasure herself.

"Goddess, Avery, I need you," he hoarsely groaned.

His guttural confession made her tighten her fingers around him. She moaned as she came, and the vibration ricocheted through him, causing him to release a raw cry as his orgasm swept through him. He was stunned by its intensity.

He reached down with a trembling hand and helped Avery to her feet, then he pulled her into his arms and held her tight. Another shudder ran through him when she wrapped her arms around his waist and hugged him back.

"Three days will never be enough, Avery," he murmured against her hair.

"Core..." she started to say.

He regretted the words the moment they slipped out. She stiffened against him, and he could sense the mental wall she was erecting between them. He tightened his arms around her and tenderly caressed her as he pressed a kiss to the top of her head.

"But, that may be all the time I have with you if I do not feed us both," he interrupted. "If I am going to keep up with you, I need sustenance."

She relaxed against him as he had hoped, and she pressed her lips to the center of his chest. He smothered a curse when she nipped him with her teeth.

She leaned her head back and grinned up at him. "In that case, I'll leave the rest of the meal preparation for you," she replied before she pressed a quick kiss to his lips.

He reluctantly released her, sliding his hand along her back as she turned away from him, and he shielded his thoughts. She was nowhere near ready to know about their unbreakable connection.

6

Night sounds filled the air as the sun set over the mountains. Stars appeared in the sky just as twinkling firebugs appeared in the forest. A soft breeze blew across the valley.

Core picked up a light blanket in case Avery became chilled. She was sitting on the lower level open deck. He strode along the platform walkway above a thick branch. It was the only access to this particular deck. Avery smiled at him when he held out the blanket.

"I was hoping you'd help keep me warm," she teased.

"The only way to keep you completely warm is to cover you with my body," he responded.

She lifted the glass of wine in her hand as he tenderly tucked the blanket around her bare legs, then sat forward so he could slide in behind her. He wrapped his arm around her waist and pulled her close so she could lean back against him.

"Here's your wine. This is incredible. I feel like I've fallen into a Johann David Wyss novel," she murmured.

He took his glass and looked at her with a confused frown. "Who is he?" he asked.

"He wrote a story called Swiss Family Robinson. It's about a family who is shipwrecked on an island. They end up building a home in a tree and fighting pirates. It was always one of my favorite stories," she explained.

He rubbed his chin against her hair and threaded his fingers through hers. "What makes this tale one of your favorites?" he asked.

She took a sip of her wine. He wasn't sure she was going to answer him at first. Over the last few months, he had learned a lot about Avery. She was not someone who shared things about herself, even something as innocent as her favorite story.

"I liked that they worked together, and they all survived," she finally replied.

There was a trace of sorrow in her voice. Unable to resist the need to comfort her, he carefully pushed against her mind—seeking entry. He was surprised when he met little resistance. He suspected the combination of wine and exhaustion was the reason.

A brief wave of guilt swept through him before he pushed it away. He would do whatever was necessary to keep her—even if it meant fighting dirty. She had pushed him away for months, refusing to allow him near her. The fact that she had come here, even with her outrageous proposition, meant that she felt the same connection with him that he felt with her. He was not above using every advantage at his disposal to keep her by his side. He only had three days to convince her that they belonged together forever, and today was almost over.

He remained focused as the faces of a man and woman flashed across her mind. They were laughing. Another image started to form, but it was quickly pushed away. The icy wall that he had grown accustomed to appeared and blocked him. He remained a shadow in her mind when her thoughts changed again. This time she was remembering them making love.

"It is so peaceful here," she sighed.

He looked across the sparkling river, seeing it through her eyes. It was easy to take for granted the things he saw every day of his life. It had always been a pleasure to live in the Eastern Mountains.

"I ran wild as a boy through these mountains. There is not a tree, cave, or river that Merrick and I have not explored. Our parents finally gave up on keeping track of where we were," he mused.

"Are... your parents still alive?" she hesitantly inquired.

Core smiled and nodded. "Yes. My father and Merrick's parents have traveled to Caldara Four to trade. My mother remained here with my younger sister," he explained. "What about you? Do your parents still live?"

"No, they died a long time ago," she answered.

He frowned when she pulled away from him and stood up. She walked over to the edge of the deck and stared out across the mountains.

He rose to his feet, his wine in one hand, the blanket in the other. She turned and held his glass of wine while he wrapped the blanket around her shoulders. She gently gave the glass back to him. For a moment they looked into each other's eyes as he stroked her fingers, then she turned around and leaned her back against his chest.

"Tomorrow, I will show you my world," he promised.

"I would like that," she said.

They stood staring out at the night. She was lost in her thoughts, and he was trying to unravel the kaleidoscope of images flashing through her mind. At one point, he moved his hand down to the long scar on her left side.

She had stopped him earlier when he tried to run his lips along the scar during their lovemaking. When he had asked her what happened, she replied that she had been in an accident when she was younger.

She grabbed his hand and pulled it away from the area. A wave of protectiveness swept through him when he felt her brief flash of intense sorrow. The accident that she'd spoken of and the death of her parents were related, he could feel that much through their connection. He would have to be patient until she was ready to share with him. He lowered his head and pressed his lips against a spot near her ear.

"We still have an hour left of the day if you are not too exhausted," he murmured with a hint of hope in his voice.

She softly snorted and turned in his arms. "Almost an hour! Well, I guess we can't let that go to waste," she replied, sliding her hand up his chest. "How would you feel about adding a little more spice this round?"

Avery moaned in her sleep. She stretched and smiled. This had to be the absolute best way in the world to wake up.

"I know you are awake," Core's deep voice murmured.

"No, I'm not. I'm having a marvelous dream," she replied.

She slowly raised her eyelids when his hand paused on her stomach. A moment later, he was leaning over her, his soft, sexy mouth inches from hers. She ran her hand up his hip and over his firm buttock.

"It can become a reality," he murmured.

She gave him a brief smile, then pushed him away. Before he could stop her, she had thrown the covers back and slid from the bed. She looked over her shoulder at him with a raised eyebrow.

"*This* is reality," she replied.

His expression hardened at her response. Turning away, she walked to the bathroom. She focused on her morning ritual, finding a measure of calm in the routine. She had finished brushing out her hair and was winding it into a ponytail when he stepped into the room.

She released a startled gasp when he wound his arm around her waist and picked her up. She looked up at their reflection in the mirror, and their gazes locked. He gave her a sharp-toothed grin.

"I have two days left of hot, mindless sex. I think it only fitting that we start the day right," he announced.

"I do love a man who honors his commitments," she purred.

Looking in the mirror, she watched as he bent his head and ran his lips along her throat. A soft moan slipped from her when she felt the scrape of his teeth. She hissed when he sank them into the curve of her neck. Her body's reaction to his bite was strange. It felt like he'd flipped a switch that heated her blood and sent her desire for him into hyper drive.

"You have no idea what you do to my insides when you bite me like this. I need to bottle whatever it is," she moaned.

His soft, warm breath swept over her skin when he chuckled. Goosebumps formed, and she moaned again as the fire built inside her. If she thought three days was going to be enough to get him out of her system, she must be nuts. She had never felt this type of intense desire for a man before.

He withdrew his teeth and ran his tongue over the mark he had left. She would have a nice assortment of marks before he was finished with her today. Thank goodness the marks faded quickly or she'd have to come up with some serious stories to explain them away. She gritted her teeth when she felt the hot flush building and her skin became super sensitive.

"You don't need to bottle it as long as I am here," he promised.

"Damn you! You know that you aren't playing fair," she groaned with a shake of her head.

His chuckle told her that he knew very well what he was doing to her. Their gazes locked in the mirror. For the first time since she'd erected the ice wall around her heart, it was beginning to melt. The fire in his eyes and the feel of his hands and mouth against her skin were threatening to break down the fortress she had created to protect herself.

"Don't, Core... don't fall in love with me," she whispered.

It is too late, Avery. You captured my heart the first moment you held your weapon to my head, his voice whispered through her mind.

She tore her gaze away from his and looked down at her hands as they gripped the edge of the sink. This is what she had been feeling inside her head—he had been there— a faint mental caress that felt so loving and masculine and... it was Core, inside her in a completely different way. She breathed in through her nose and slowly turned to face him.

The burning need inside her was growing along with the despair. She embraced the first emotion and hoped that she hid the second. Lifting up on her toes, she pulled his head down to her for a kiss that begged him to just accept what they had now.

7

Several hours later, they were standing along the edge of a meadow. He had been showing Avery more of his world, hoping that she would love it as much as he did. He watched her pile her hair up in a messy pony tail. Her windblown hair made her look wild and free, a stark contrast to the composed woman he'd first met.

His eyes darkened when the thin fabric of her blouse stretched across her breasts. He could see the dark circle of her areolas and her taut nipples through the material. She glanced at him in amusement when he moaned.

"I should have worn a bra. I decided it would be more of a hassle than it was worth because every time I put one on, you take it off," she teased.

He grinned at her. "It is fun to remove it, but I enjoy feeling your hard nipples against my back," he admitted.

She stopped in front of him. "Is that why you didn't wear a shirt? I thought it was because you liked my hands on you," she retorted with a raised eyebrow.

He reached out and grabbed her hand, raising it to his lips and pressing a kiss to the center of the intricate circles of her bond mark.

Then he touched it with the tip of his tongue. Her loud gasp told him she felt what he was doing at the center of her being.

"I am not even going to try to understand what just happened," she said with a shake of her head. "Where are you taking me to next?"

He tucked a stray strand of her hair behind her ear and caressed her cheek before he pulled her toward his land glider. A mischievous glint flared in his eyes.

"Would you like to control the glider?" he asked.

Her eyes lit up with delight. "I wondered how long it would take for you to finally offer me a chance," she replied with a grin.

He laughed when she eagerly pulled him toward the land glider. The craft was a simple machine that allowed his people to move quickly through the dense forest. Avery called it a floating motorcycle. He remembered seeing a motorcycle when he was on her world. It seemed much more dangerous than the land glider.

He waited as Avery climbed on before he sat down behind her, wrapping one hand around her waist and another over her unbound breast while he leaned forward to rest his chin on her shoulder.

She tilted her head to the side and gave him a pointed look. He just grinned in response. She shook her head.

"Is copping a feel the only reason you are letting me drive?" she asked, turning her attention to the controls.

"Yes," he replied.

She released an inelegant snort. "Well, hold me tight," she advised.

Core tightened his hold on her as she started the transport. He should have known she had carefully watched what he had been doing all morning. In seconds, they were hovering in the air.

He slid his hands down to her waist when she leaned forward, and the glider smoothly accelerated, picking up speed as Avery became more confident in how to control it.

They wove their way through the forest, moving to a higher elevation. He gazed around at the massive trees and pride surged through him at the beauty of his homeland. The Eastern Clan had settled throughout this area when the forest was still young. His people nurtured and protected it, and it gave them plentiful food, shelter, and protection in return.

When they weren't all crowded into Tilly's marathon movie event, his clan moved among the trees like ghosts, and the birds and plants warned them if strangers entered their domain. He scowled at the memory of the deceitful human male, Scott Bachman, they'd found here. He had been the first to tell the clan that humans could bond with the Prime, and he had caused far too much suffering before he was stopped.

"How do you know Scott Bachman?" Avery asked with surprise.

Core blinked. It was too much to hope that Avery felt connected enough to him right now to hear his thoughts. He must have spoken the man's name out loud. He grimaced with distaste, wishing they could talk about something else.

As Cosmos' security officer, Avery probably knew part of this story. She would certainly know that Hannah and Tink were the eldest and youngest daughters of Tilly and Angus, that Tink had been the first human to go through Cosmos' gateway, that Hannah was the second, and that Tink and Hannah were the bond mates of J'kar and Borj, the eldest and second eldest sons of Teriff 'Tag Krell Manok, the leader of Baade, and his bond mate Tresa.

"He was not a good human," he responded.

Avery shot him a quick look. "No shit, but that still doesn't explain how you know about him. Is he here?" she asked.

Core shook his head. "He is dead. He was brought here after he almost killed Tink on your world. He killed two guards before escaping into the forest. We found him. We would have killed him immediately, but he offered us something we couldn't refuse—hope. Not long after, he and two outcasts from our clan kidnapped Hannah. They are dead now too," he added in a blunt tone.

"What happened to Hannah?" Avery quietly asked, slowing down the glider.

He tightened his arms around her waist. "She was hurt, but has since recovered. Borj is very attentive to her and their children. I know you think it is a terrible thing to be the bond mate of a Prime,

Avery, but not all Prime are bad. It has been difficult with so few women among our kind. For years, our people have searched nearby worlds to find a mate who would complete us. We lost hope as it seemed certain our species would die out," he continued.

"There are other planets near you with people? That's right; you said your father was on a trip. It's hard to wrap my head around all of this sometimes," she mused, shaking her head in disbelief.

"Turn to the northwest. There is a place I would like to show you," he instructed before he continued. "There are many different species. "The Prime are the most powerful because our technology is more advanced. You have only seen a small portion of my world, and the village where I live may appear simple, but it relies on very complex technology. We sustainably make the most of our natural resources to provide abundance, protection, and joy to everyone," he shared.

"I've seen your home. It is unbelievable," she said.

"When you pass through the trees here, there will be a cliff," he warned.

He straightened as she maneuvered the land glider between the trees and onto a wide rock shelf. She powered down the glider and he disembarked. As she stepped off the transport, he reached out and grasped her hand, steadying her.

They silently walked to the edge of the cliff. Below was a vast, deep gorge. Waterfalls flowed over the sides. Some plunged hundreds of feet while others were like steps as they cascaded down into several large basins until reaching the wide river below.

"This is beautiful. It reminds me of the Grand Canyon back home. I wonder if the Colorado River once looked like this as it cut through the canyon," she murmured.

He stepped up behind her and wrapped his arms around her waist, then he pointed to the series of falls closest to them. She turned her head to look at them.

"The falls supply power to our village and to the security grid for this region. There are many such power stations, built to blend in with the natural surroundings. We did not want to ruin what the Goddess gave us by trying to tame the flow, and the natural fall of the water hides our infrastructure from anyone foolish enough to attack us," he explained.

Avery shook her head in wonder. "Smart. On my world, the first things an invading force attacks are the communication and power structures. Divide and conquer: create chaos and move in to take over. It's a classic military strategy," she said.

He looked down at her with a raised eyebrow. "You have studied military strategies?" he asked.

"Some. My job is to keep Cosmos Raines Industries safe from attacks. Obviously, Cosmos does more than run a corporation full of computer nerds. We sometimes go into the most hostile places on Earth looking for the worst of those who prey upon the weak. Avilov was one of them. You saw what he was capable of. The people who took Merrick are targets too. We took down some, but there are still key figures that remain free: Markham, Wright, and Dolinski. I shouldn't have come here, but with Merrick safe on your world now..." her voice faded and she shrugged. "I decided the world would have to survive without me for three days."

Core made a soft sound of acknowledgment as he breathed in her scent and basked in her warmth. "I would not have wished Merrick's captivity on him..." he mused, "but if it wasn't for everything that had happened, I would not have met you," he grudgingly admitted.

"How is he doing?" Avery asked, tilting her head back against his shoulder to look up at him.

He gazed out over the canyon to hide his expression. After so long trying to temper the volatility of the desperate men in his clan, attempting to contain his own emotions was second nature, though it was difficult when he thought of how close to death Merrick had been. He took a breath and told himself that it was important to be calm. This relationship between humans and the Prime was new and therefore delicate. He did not want her to think that he blamed all humans for what had happened to Merrick.

"The drugs almost killed him," he finally said, "and his recovery is slow. Now that he is awake, he is impatient to return to your world. He has found his bond mate."

Avery chuckled and shook her head. "Poor woman!" she teased, turning in his arms.

Core smiled and caressed her cheek. "And yet, finding our bond mate makes us the richest warriors in all the world," he softly countered.

The amusement in Avery's eyes faded and was replaced by a haunted look that he wanted more than anything to chase away. He could almost see the barrier that blocked him from her mind. It was like an empty vortex, sucking the light away and leaving nothing but darkness. He kept his hand on her cheek and focused on her thoughts.

"Don't!" her sharp command and the mental push she gave him felt like a blow.

"Avery…" he murmured in concern.

She took a step away from him, her expression accusing, then she turned and walked back to the glider. He followed her, and when she climbed on, he noticed her knuckles were white where she gripped the handles.

"I don't want to end this with regret, Core. I want us to remember the beautiful time we had together. No strings, no expectations, no demands…" she said, looking at him with dark eyes that revealed more emotion than she probably realized.

"Just three days of mindless, never-ending sex," he said in a soft voice.

She gave him a crooked smile, but her eyes held a hint of grief. "And each other's company," she quietly finished.

He reached down and brushed a kiss along her upturned lips, then lifted his hands and framed her face, quietly studying her features before he brushed another kiss to the end of her nose.

"Would you like to swim in a magical cave?" he asked.

Her low, sexy laugh was a relief, and he climbed onto the glider, wrapping his arms tightly around her waist. She leaned back against him for a moment before firing up the glider. They rose into the air. She looked over her shoulder and raised an eyebrow.

"Who wouldn't want to see a magical cave on an alien world? Life doesn't get much better than this," she informed him.

He smiled wickedly and slid his hands up under the fabric of her shirt to her unbound breasts. She gasped as he cupped them.

"I can think of something that might," he murmured in her ear.

He laughed when she cursed and pressed harder on the glider's accelerator. Her delighted laughter soon mixed with his as they sped through the forest. His heart swelled with love.

Whether Avery would admit it or not, they were made for each other. He would not be giving up without a fight—and not just because the unaccepted bond would eventually kill him, as it would any Prime. He wouldn't *want* to live without her. If there was no way to be with Avery and he had a choice about whether to live or die, Core would have found a way to end his suffering.

8

Avery rolled onto her back and floated in the water. She looked up through the opening in the ceiling of the cave. The stars were beginning to come out. The walls of the cave glowed with lustrous colors.

"This is so beautiful. You were right. It is magical," she murmured.

Core treaded water next to her. She could feel his eyes on her instead of the cave. She lowered her legs and turned toward him. Winding her arms around his neck and her legs around his waist, she let him keep both of them afloat.

"I could watch you all day long, every day, as you learn more about my world, and never grow tired of seeing the joy reflected in your eyes," he said.

Avery's throat tightened with emotion. She slid her hands up and cupped his face. For a moment, she did nothing more. She wanted to burn the vision of him in her mind; his wet hair in disarray from their swim, his strong face relaxed, and his silver-colored eyes burning with the familiar flames of desire and another emotion she was afraid to attach a name to.

She caressed his bottom lip with her thumb, then slowly leaned forward and gently pressed her lips to his. This time the emotion behind the kiss was not raw passion but something deeper. It felt bittersweet.

He parted his lips and they deepened the kiss, forgetting the world around them. For just a moment, time stood still. There was no past, no future—just this one moment in time where they were together.

Avery closed her eyes and tried to hold onto the strange emotions overwhelming her. In her mind, she could see a web of delicately thin silver threads piercing the wall of ice she kept around her heart. It felt warm and safe. She opened her eyes and looked into his mesmerizing ones for a long moment. Then she leaned forward and pressed her cheek to his.

Don't fall in love with me. Please don't fall in love with me, she silently begged.

He tightened his arms around her and held her as if he would never let her go. They remained like that for several minutes before he loosened his arms and released her. They swam back to the shallow end of the pool and she threaded her fingers through his.

"You know, I think I've spent more time these past couple of days getting dressed and undressed than I ever have in the past year!" she softly laughed as she bent over to pick up a towel.

"I would be very happy if you wanted to forgo the getting dressed part," he teased.

"Funny, I was thinking the same thing about you," she retorted.

She ran an appreciative gaze over Core's muscular form. Damn if the man didn't make her want to permanently give up wearing clothes. His low rumbling growl and obvious physical response, which was growing harder right before her eyes, told her that he was well aware of her thoughts.

Ten minutes later, she was wrapping her arms around Core's waist and leaning against his back as he drove the glider back through the forest toward his home. She pressed her cheek against his shoulder and sighed deeply in contentment. The forest was as beautiful at night as it was during the day. Several times she swore she caught a glimpse of something moving in the shadows.

"There are many different beasts that live within the forest. They know to stay away if they wish to live another day," Core explained over the hum of the glider.

She rested her chin on his shoulder. "You're in my head again. I can feel you there, you know," she dryly observed.

He shook with silent laughter. "Do you want to feel more of me?" he challenged.

She reached down between his legs and squeezed. His laughter echoed through the night, drowning out the other sounds with its rich tone. She smiled and held him tight.

It didn't take them nearly as long as she'd thought it would to return to Core's home. She reluctantly released her hold on him as they came to a stop, and she dismounted the glider, then picked up the things they had carried with them on their adventures today.

Core activated the shield over the glider and took some of the items from her grasp. They walked over to the entrance, and she looked up when he held her hand.

"I had a wonderful day," she said.

He lifted her hand to his lips and pressed a kiss to her knuckles. "There is much more to show you. We have many beautiful cities here, and while my village has been quiet, tomorrow most of the residents will return. I've become spoiled the last two days having it and you to myself," he replied.

He released her hand and activated the lift. She didn't reply to his unspoken desire that she stay much longer. There was no way she could remain. She already knew this had been a mistake.

Her plan to get Core out of her system while keeping her emotions under control had been a miserable failure. She didn't think she would ever get enough of him, and she didn't want to think about the pain she would inevitably feel when she left. She was emotionally invested—after a lifetime of fighting attachment to anything and anyone.

"Why don't we shower, then prepare some dinner?" he suggested.

She nodded. "I'll take these up and put them in the cleansing unit," she said.

"I'll be there in a moment," he added with a grin.

Avery stepped to the side when the doors opened and watched as he walked out of the lift and onto the main level. She closed her eyes and leaned her head against the wall when the doors closed behind him. This was going to be so much harder than she'd expected.

She opened her eyes when the doors opened again, this time on the top floor. Stepping out of the lift, she turned to the right and headed for the cleansing room. Inside, she opened the alien version of a washer/dryer combo and dropped their damp clothing and towels inside. She quickly stripped out of her clothes and placed them inside as well, then she walked toward the shower.

Warm jets of water automatically turned on when she stepped inside. She bowed her head as the water flowed over her, and slowly opened her hand to study the intricate circles in the center of her palm.

Cosmos had warned her, but she hadn't believed him. She carefully traced the pattern. The center of her palm grew warm and for a moment she thought she could see the glimmer of silver threads reaching toward the door of the cleansing room.

She blinked and looked up when she heard Core enter the room. He had already removed his clothes and was dropping them into the cleansing unit. He shut the compartment and activated the unit, but his eyes were on her.

She daringly caressed the mark on her palm as she looked into his intense silver eyes, trembling at his reaction to her. Physically, he was hard and ready and magnificent, but it was his mental reaction to her caress that shook her the most.

"You can't continue to ignore our connection, Avery," he murmured as he stepped into the shower with her.

Avery pressed her fingers against his lips. She didn't want to talk. She didn't want to try to understand everything that was happening—tomorrow would come all too soon. Tomorrow would be their last day together.

He shook his head back and forth ever so slightly beneath her touch. She moved her finger away from his lips to caress his cheek, and slid her other hand up his arm. Her breath caught when his calloused hands moved over her wet skin and drew her close.

Their kiss held the same passion it had the last two days, but it also tasted of desperation and despair. She felt his swift denial as it swept through her mind, and she parted her lips under the pressure of his kiss.

Open your mind to me.

Avery stiffened for a moment before she acquiesced to his demand. Opening her mind to him was easier than she'd expected. In some ways, the thought of being able to communicate with another person like this was terrifying; but, at the same time, it was exhilarating.

Feel me. See me. Touch me, he encouraged as he deepened their kiss.

~

Core tightened his arms around Avery when he felt her relax the tight control she kept over her mind. He swore she had more self-discipline than any of the fiercest warriors he had ever known. Even though she was lowering her protective walls, he could sense there was a part of herself that she continued to hide. He ended their kiss, pulling back and resting his forehead against hers. Her eyes were closed, and her mind was filled with only the things she wanted to share.

Memories slowly opened to him. He saw fuzzy, bright glimpses of the humans he had met when he was on Earth. He closed his eyes and focused. The images became clear. He saw members of Cosmos' team and felt the pride Avery had in their determination to make their world a better place.

She had created a mental structure like a stage with these memories in the spotlight, but just outside that light he could sense, just barely, a darker side of her life, a place where she moved like a ghost, unable to touch and afraid to be touched.

He gently traced the thin scar along her left hip where a bullet had grazed her, and another along her shoulder caused by a knife. The

her tongue along his teeth, and Core parted his lips, emitting a loud, deep growl in response.

The slight taste of copper filled his senses, and he knew that his razor-sharp teeth had cut her. The wound would heal almost instantly thanks to his saliva, but it was enough to send him over the edge.

He pushed up inside her as far as he could go, bent his head, and bit her, piercing the soft flesh along the column of her neck. She screamed in white hot pleasure and stiffened in his arms. He held her immobilized while he rocked his hips harder and faster. They were locked together in mind and body, their hearts frantically beating as one, their emotions and physical excitement surging unfettered between them, exponentially magnifying what they each felt.

"Core... Yes, now.... Yesssss..." Avery moaned as her control shattered and her inner muscles greedily clutched his shaft. Core relished the intensity of Avery's release, and as her tight sheath clamped down around his cock, the tingling that had started earlier spread until his whole body burned with it.

In pulsing waves, he gave his seed to her. He pulled his teeth from her flesh and tilted his head back. A hoarse cry was ripped from his throat when the wave crested, and he ground his hips against her.

He held Avery tightly to him and pressed her back against the wall. Her arms were wrapped around his neck, and her head rested against his shoulder.

They stayed locked together for several minutes before he carefully withdrew from her, and she lowered her feet to the floor. Even then, they clung to each other to keep from melting to the floor of the shower as their legs threatened to give out.

"I think we're getting to the mindless, endless part of the weekend," she murmured against his flesh.

He chuckled at the sound of exhaustion in her voice. Turning his head, he pressed a kiss to the top of her wet hair before he gently tilted her head back. She closed her eyes to keep the water out of them. He leaned down and brushed another kiss across her lips.

"Let me wash you," he murmured.

Her lips twitched, and she nodded. "Go right ahead. I honestly don't think I have the strength to do it myself at the moment," she replied.

"For once, I have you completely under my control," he teased.

Her eyelids fluttered, and she lowered her head far enough to give him an amused look and a raised eyebrow. Her lips quirked suddenly and her eyes sparkled before she retorted, "Hardly. You might have noticed you're the one catering to me, not the other way around. The way I see it, I have you under my control," she announced with a royal wave of her hand.

He chuckled, picked up the washcloth and soap, and knelt in front of her. "Then I bow at your feet, my lady," he acquiesced.

She gasped as he tenderly moved the rough, soapy washcloth over her sensitive labia and clit. "Damn, but I could get used to this," she moaned.

I could as well. It does not have to end tomorrow, Avery. This could be the beginning, he silently replied.

He knew she'd heard him, but she refused to respond. Someday she would, though—when she was ready. Now that she had opened to him, he would always be a faint presence in her mind. He privately swore he would not make her regret giving him a way in, but he was not going to let her shut him out again either. The agreed upon three days *were* just the beginning; he was sure of it.

9

Houston, Texas:

As Karl Markham slowly walked toward the booth, he noted that the restaurant was small and decorated with a wide assortment of what some interior designer would probably have called New Age Art Deco. In the corner, a man was strumming out songs on his guitar about love, war, and finding a voice in the sea of faces. He passed the booth, sticking the adhesive side of his dime-sized listening device to the underside of the table as he went by. He continued on to the bathroom without pause.

A few minutes later, Karl was sliding into another of the quaint restaurant booths and picked up the menu the waitress had placed on the table in front of him. He scanned the unappetizing menu, then idly looked out the window, watching the people strolling along the brightly lighted streets. Most were enjoying the break from the suffocating heat of the day. A late afternoon shower followed by a cold front had cooled things down. The evening was filled with couples and people hoping to hook up. He was here for an entirely different reason.

"What would you like to drink?" the waitress asked, pausing by his table.

"Water, no ice, and the steak," he ordered.

The waitress wrinkled her nose. "The new chef just added that to the menu. How do you want it cooked?" she asked.

"Rare. I'll take the potato fully loaded and Ranch on the side for my salad," he requested, handing her the menu.

He sat back when she moved to the table behind him and listened as four women ordered. Three of them ordered salad while the fourth one mumbled something he couldn't quite catch. Reaching into his jacket, he increased the volume of the earbud in his right ear so he could better hear the conversation.

"So, what do you think Avery is up to? She's been all secretive and super-focused lately," Maria Garcia asked.

"She went to Cosmos' warehouse in Calais. She said she was taking a vacation," Trudy Wilson chuckled.

"A vacation! Avery? Does she even know what one is?" Maria exclaimed in surprise.

"She does when it involves a huge-ass alien that has been trying to get her number for the last six months," Rose Caine dryly replied.

"You shouldn't talk about that stuff here," the fourth woman, the one he hadn't recognized, muttered in a barely audible voice.

"Amelia's right. Someone might hear us," Rose replied.

"So, who thinks the Cowboys have a chance at winning this coming Sunday?" Trudy said.

Karl looked up when the waitress came with his glass of water.

Over the next two hours, he listened to three out of the four women talk about everything from football to world politics while he ate his dinner. The fourth one didn't speak unless she was asked a direct question and usually responded with a shrug, nod, or the minimum amount of words. He finished his meal and paid for it, delaying until the women finally stood up to leave. He watched the fourth woman as she walked away. He couldn't see her face. She wore a large hat pulled down low and an oversized black coat.

A sense of unease ran through him when he saw her deliberately drop something on the floor. She glanced around the room as she brought her booted foot down onto the silver disk. He winced when his earbud loudly screeched in his ear.

Her gaze locked on his face for a brief moment before she turned and hurried after the other women. He pulled the earpiece from his ear and slid it into his pocket, then he rose from his seat and walked over to the silver disk. He stooped and picked up the broken remains of the listening device.

Wrapping his fingers around the device, he hurriedly threaded his way between the tables and out of the restaurant. He looked both ways, and clenched his fist when he couldn't see where the women had gone. He needed more information—especially about the woman called Amelia.

Karl turned and started walking back toward his car. The back of his neck tingled, and he stepped into the shadowed doorway of a closed store. He scanned the area.

He was sure he was being followed. That was almost funny. It wasn't often that the predator became the prey. The feeling passed after several minutes. He saw nothing out of the ordinary in the crowd.

He was about to step back out when he saw the darkly clothed woman from the restaurant standing across the street. She was staring intensely in his direction, trying to see into the shadows where he had disappeared. He smiled. This one was smart.

A large, noisy group passed his doorway, and Karl matched their pace, blending in with the crowd. At the corner, he parted ways with the happy party and headed for his car. It was parked several blocks away.

Ten minutes later he merged into traffic. The leads had come full circle back to Cosmos Raines Industries. They were the link to the alien Karl had captured.

His work for Keiser was finished, but who could let something like this go? The research doctor had her chance to experiment on the alien, and now Dr. Margaret Rockman and a handful of men hired to safeguard the project were dead. It was Raines who had interfered. To find his missing alien, it was only logical to follow those who knew where he was—and these women appeared to have that information.

Karl was pulling into the circular entrance of the hotel he was staying in when his cell phone vibrated. He reached down and pulled it out of his pocket. A quick glance at the screen identified the caller.

"Yes?" he asked in a terse voice.

"The men I hired to bring in the alien's girlfriend are dead. There are police all over the building," Weston Wright answered.

"And the alien?" he demanded.

"I heard an old woman telling one of the police officers that Banks' had an unusual man with her," Weston replied.

"And you don't know where they are now. Where are *you* now?" Karl asked his half-brother.

"Still in Portland," Weston replied.

Karl thought for a moment. "My flight gets in at nine tomorrow morning. Pick me up at the airport," he ordered.

"Do you know where she might be going?" Weston asked.

"Yes. I'll tell you tomorrow," he replied before he ended the call.

Several minutes later, his car was valeted and Karl was in his penthouse room, standing in front of the windows that overlooked Houston's downtown. In the distance, he could see the glowing dark red sign on CRI 's corporate high rise.

His thoughts returned to Addie Banks. It had taken Weston three days to locate her due to the seized records. She had only been working at Keiser for a few days as a custodian. She was single, deaf, and working her way through school. There was nothing to indicate that she was cooperating with CRI, the police, or the government. She had just been in the wrong place, at the wrong time, and had seen too much.

Karl looked down at the cell phone in his hand. Pressing a series of numbers, he waited until the call was answered by an airline agent and he ordered a plane ticket to Portland for the next morning. Once the ticket had been purchased, he made another call.

"Digs," the deep male voice said.

"I need equipment," Karl curtly replied.

"Account," Digs said.

"KM185," Karl answered.

"What do you need, sir?" Digs asked, his tone suddenly cautious.

Karl smirked. Money and power could buy anything—but fear gave a man the edge he needed for complete control.

He calmly gave his order, knowing it would be delivered to his half-brother by the time he arrived. Digs repeated the list of weapons that Karl had requested along with a delivery time. Once his purchase was completed, Karl slid his cell phone back into his pocket.

Turning away from the window, he pulled the chair out from the desk, sat down, opened his laptop, and logged in. In minutes, he was scanning the encrypted files of the CIA database, searching for all the information he could find about Avery Lennox and Amelia. A heated curse slipped from his lips when he was alerted that the files he'd been trying to access had triggered a location search. He quickly abandoned his research, closing down the laptop. A thoughtful frown creased his brow. It appeared that CRI was hiding more than just aliens.

"What else is there that you don't want the rest of the world to know about?" he mulled, swiveling in his chair to stare at CRI's high rise.

Seaside, Oregon

The gas pump clicked off, and Karl replaced the hose, glancing up as Weston walked toward him with a grin on his face. The three boys that Weston had been talking to looked excited. Each boy was dressed in dark gear and was carrying a backpack. Karl could see different colored splatters on their clothing.

"What's that about?" Karl asked.

"I recruited some extra help to create a diversion. They are going to shoot up the house and draw Merrick away. I told them we had a friend staying there and wanted to play a practical joke on him," Weston said, opening the passenger door.

"And they believed you?" Karl asked.

"Are you kidding? All I had to do was wave a hundred dollar bill and promise another one when they were finished and those boys were willing to do anything I asked," Weston gloated.

Karl tightened his mouth in annoyance. "This could complicate matters. I told you I didn't want to bring anyone else in on this," he said, opening his door and sliding into the driver's seat.

Weston followed him in, and shut his door. "I've seen what that alien can do more than you have. Shoot the kids if they get in your way, but I'm not taking any chances. I'll give you a word of advice. If you get a clear shot to kill the bastard—take it. He isn't some fucking moron that will shit his pants if he knows you are hunting him. This guy will relish the battle and not stop until he has either won or is dead," he replied.

Karl started the car. "Oh, I understand exactly who and what kind of predator he is, *little brother*. I also know exactly where I'm going to mount his body when I'm done playing with him," he responded.

Weston didn't respond. Karl knew his brother. Weston was weak. He would rather hide behind someone else than risk his own neck. Weston also knew that Karl wouldn't hesitate to leave him behind if it was necessary.

Weston had been right in his assessment of the alien. That was what fascinated him the most. He relished the opportunity to pit his own wits and cunning against someone he considered almost his equal.

A half hour later, Karl turned onto the long road that led to the Banks' cottage. The house was situated between the ocean on the west and a lake on the east. He slowed down as they passed the neighbor's house on the corner. The shutters over the windows were closed, and the driveway was littered with leaves. It seemed no one was staying there at the moment. Karl parked in front.

"See if you can find evidence of anyone at the Banks' cottage," he ordered.

Weston picked up a pair of binoculars from between the seats and rolled down his window. Karl scanned the area in front of him, picking out places where he could set up. A moment later, Weston lowered the binoculars to his lap and rolled the window back up.

"It's her car," Weston replied.

"I'll circle around, and we'll park near the house at the end of the road. When did you tell those boys to come?" he asked.

Karl listened as Weston outlined his plan. The boys would shoot their paintball guns and draw Merrick out. Karl would then shoot the alien with a tranquilizer while Weston went inside and had fun with Addie Banks. Then they would enact Karl's plan to take her with them, and leave the alien there with a map showing where to find Addie—or what remained of her by the time Weston was done with her. Karl knew from the tests performed on the alien that the man had an advanced sense of smell and would recognize what had occurred while he was unconscious.

Weston wasn't excited about any part of the plan except his time with Addie. Karl had always liked a challenge more than his half-brother, and there was nothing like the rush of hunting a hurting, desperate creature that knew it was about to die. Karl wasn't stupid, though. He realized that the alien was a very dangerous beast unlike anything or anyone he had ever hunted before. Because of that, he would take extra precautions to ensure that he had the advantage. The hunt would be in a setting that he controlled.

10

A slight smile curved Avery's lips when she saw that Core had also fallen asleep. Between their explorations and the sex, they had both been tired. She lay on her side and stared at Core's relaxed face until thirst drove her from the bed.

She silently rolled to the side and stood up, grabbing the oversized shirt that she normally slept in as she walked toward the door. A quick glance showed that it was still dark outside.

She exited the room, sliding the shirt over her head as she made her way down to the kitchen on the lower level. She lightly trailed her hand along the polished wood railing as she descended.

The clock on the kitchen wall showed that it wasn't even midnight yet. The sudden realization of how quickly the last two days had flown hit her hard. The clan would be returning tomorrow. It would be best if she were gone before then. Avery didn't want to draw unnecessary attention to Core. She had promised him three days, but spending another full day here wouldn't be smart.

Avery leaned forward and gripped the end of the counter as a wave of agonizing loss coursed through her, reminding her so clearly of that day so long ago, the day she kept locked away in a box in her mind. She took in a shuddering breath and willed the feeling away.

"What happened that day that causes you so much pain, Avery?" Core asked.

She stiffened at the soft sound of Core's voice and blindly stared at the kitchen cabinet in front of her. She hadn't heard him come into the room. The muscle in her jaw throbbed as she fought to tamp down her emotions. The life of the man who had destroyed her family had been *hers* to take, so she had never talked about him or about that day—not to the agents, not to the psychiatrist assigned to her, not her handler—no one. Now the words tumbled out as if she was unable to contain them any longer.

"My parents were spies—and when needed, assassins—for two opposing governments. They were the best of the best at what they did. Only their handlers and a very small group of politicians knew who they were. Things were heating up between their respective governments. It was suspected that a third country was working with several terrorist organizations to escalate the tension. My mother was sent in to observe and report back on the threat," she said in a monotone voice.

"What happened?" Core asked.

His voice sounded closer than it had been, and a moment later she felt the warmth of his body against her and his hands on her hips. She resisted leaning back against him at first but finally gave in.

"She met my father. He had been sent in by his country to do the same thing. Things turned nasty, and they ended up helping each other escape. They fell in love... and then had me," she quietly added.

He tightened his arms around her and pressed a kiss to the top of her head. She released her grip on the counter and laid her hands over his arms.

She was surprised at the sense of peace that came over her as she related her story. For the first time, she was seeing the situation from a different angle—her parents. Before, it had been difficult for her to understand why they would risk so much for a personal dream. Her feelings for Core gave her a new insight into not only their lives, but her own.

"It was very difficult for you—and lonely," he reflected.

She laughed harshly and bowed her head. "You're in my head," she commented.

"Yes," he replied.

She appreciated that he didn't try to lie or make excuses. Her throat tightened as it always did when she remembered that day the past had caught up with her parents. She closed her eyes and released her grip on the mental wall she had constructed to keep the memories locked away.

Core held her close. He seemed surprised that she wasn't resisting him, and she couldn't really blame him. She was surprised herself. For some reason, she wanted to share this with him. Perhaps a small part of her knew it was safe to do so—it wasn't like it would make any difference.

She leaned her head back against him and let the memories come with every tiny detail vividly relived. He saw her naïve excitement, her fierce competitive nature, and felt the love of her parents. He also lived through the agonizing physical pain and the more devastating emotional one as she watched a young girl's life sucked away and knew Kassy was simply collateral damage. She had been in the wrong place at the wrong time—near Avery.

"Sweet Goddess, Avery," Core murmured.

He was reliving the moment the bullet ripped through her flesh and burned a path through her tender organs. The seeping of blood soaking the ground around her and the cries of a distraught mother had become mere distractions as she witnessed the assassination of her parents. Only then had the screams punctured her awareness, and she'd realized that she was close to joining her parents.

She would have given up if the man hadn't turned and looked at her. Their eyes had locked for a moment, and in that split second, it was her desire for revenge that had kept her alive.

"What did you do?"

Avery opened her eyes and stared down at the counter. "When I was seventeen, I began searching for him. I was nineteen when I located him in Berlin. I hunted him down and executed him with the same calculated indifference that he used when he killed my parents and Kassy. My only regret was that I could only do it once," she stated.

"For us, it is called the Right of Justice. If you and he had been on Prime, we would have facilitated the confrontation. It was your right to face the man who did this to you and your family," Core stated without an ounce of judgement.

She turned in his arms. "I'm not a nice person, Core. Don't make the mistake of thinking that I am. What I did had nothing to do with justice and everything to do with revenge. Under the right circumstances, I could slit your throat and walk away without a backwards glance," she stated, staring unblinking into his eyes.

"She could do it, too," a sultry woman's voice murmured behind Core. "I always wondered what happened, Avery. I'm so sorry about your parents and Kassy,"

"What are you doing here, RITA2?" Avery demanded.

"Warning you that Teriff, Derik, and Hendrik are at the front door. It appears the council has been busy deciding that they absolutely must see Merrick tomorrow. You'd think Tilly having a film festival would have distracted the old bastards," RITA2 said with a sigh.

"Merrick knows they want to see him. He will contact RITA to open the portal after he finds Addie," Core said.

Avery frowned. "You didn't tell me he returned to Earth," she said.

Core grinned. "I was distracted. Besides, there was no stopping him," he explained.

"It's too dangerous for him to be back there," she growled in annoyance.

There were still three main threats that had not been contained. It was more than conceivable that one or possibly all three still on the loose would search for Addie Banks to get to Merrick. God, she was stupid! When Core mentioned that Merrick had a bond mate on Earth, Avery should have immediately ordered security for the woman—and she shouldn't have come here until she had Markham, Wright, and Dolinski's bodies in a bag. Avery pushed Core out of the way when Core's home computer system also announced that they had visitors.

"I'll go get dressed," she said as she walked away from him.

After a few moments, she heard Core's deep voice growling at his visitors, then she was too far away to hear anything else. Once she was back in their bedroom, she pulled off her nightshirt, grabbed a change of clothes out of her bag, and went into the bathroom. She put the clothes on the counter and stepped into the shower.

Five minutes later she exited the shower and dried herself. Her thoughts were on everything she needed to do when she returned. If RITA sent her to their location, maybe she could keep the Gateway open until Avery could drop-kick the huge alien and his girlfriend back through it.

Avery put on her panties and bra, stepped into a pair of tan dress slacks and fastened them. Bending over, she brushed her hair and pulled the dark brown strands up into a ponytail. She grabbed her blouse off the counter and pulled it on, buttoning it as she walked through RITA2's holographic body into the room.

"Core is right, Avery, I have researched the man who murdered your parents, and he was truly an evil human being. Even his handlers expressed concern about his mental stability, but their superiors wanted him to continue working. That program was eventually shut down, in large part because of you," RITA2 said.

Avery paused. This was the reason she had been so careful to hide her background. Once RITA or RITA2 had even a small piece of information, the AI supercomputers would search through millions of databases worldwide—*Earth-wide,* Avery silently corrected—until they had located, processed, and analyzed all the relevant data—and then the RITAs would proceed to 'help' however they saw fit.

Avery turned and looked at RITA2. The hologram was dressed in a style similar to Avery's, with white slacks and an emerald green blouse that matched her eyes. For a moment, Avery felt like she was looking at a living person before she shook her head.

"Delete the information from your systems, RITA2, or I will," Avery ordered in a low, frosty tone.

Avery watched as RITA2's eyes flickered before returning to normal. "All information has been deleted," RITA2 replied.

"Good," Avery answered, turning back to her bag.

She pulled her weapons out and strapped one knife to her arm under her sleeve, and the other knife to her calf under her slacks. She carefully checked each gun out of habit to make sure the clips were full before tucking one into the holster at the small of her back. She picked up her short, black leather jacket from the chair by the bed, shrugged into it, and put her other gun into the pocket, then calmly packed the rest of her personal items in the bag.

"Oh dear," RITA2 murmured, her eyes suddenly glowing.

Avery looked up and frowned. "What is it?" she asked.

"My sis just connected to tell me that Trudy has been shot and Merrick has asked for our help," RITA2 explained, her eyes still glowing.

She turned when Core suddenly appeared, his face grim. "You know about the situation?" he asked.

Avery nodded and watched as Core kicked off his loose pants and reached into a drawer to pull out a black uniform.

"Debrief us, RITA2," Avery ordered.

"Merrick went through a portal to Earth the day before you arrived here. RITA tells me the Portland police are investigating two currently unidentified men's deaths in Addie's apartment and her disappearance. Merrick and Addie are currently in her family cottage in Seaside, Oregon. Trudy tried to warn Merrick and Addie that Markham and Wright would know about the cottage. Trudy has been shot. The extent of her injuries is currently unknown, but she is alive. DAR informed Teriff, Derik, Hendrick, and Core of the situation. The other three are outside retrieving weapons from their transport. I'm afraid information is mostly limited to what was discussed before Trudy arrived and the phone call RITA received from Merrick," RITA2 said with an apologetic smile. "I'll program your Gateway device to the location, and once you are through, my sister will program it to bring you to the medical wing of the 'Tag Krell Manok palace."

"Let's go," Core said as he slid a long, deadly blade into a sheath at his waist, grabbed the silver cylinder that Avery knew was the Gateway device from a drawer, and took her by the arm.

They entered the lift. In seconds, they were stepping outside. Two of the men sent her an inquisitive glance while the third frowned at her before turning a dark, disapproving look on Core. She recognized Teriff 'Tag Krell Manok, the leader of Baade, from the dossier that RITA had compiled for her.

"What is she doing here?" Teriff demanded.

"Vacation," Avery shot back.

"Vacation?" Teriff repeated with a frown.

"It's a long story, Teriff," Core added.

"RITA2, open the Gateway," Avery ordered, checking her gun to make sure the safety was off before looking at RITA2.

Core swung his arm out and blocked her. "Let me go through first," he murmured.

Avery opened her mouth to protest, but then took one look at Core and nodded in agreement. Core's features were hard now. All signs of the gentle lover were gone, and in his place was a ruthless, alien, killing machine. She looked at the other three men. Their expressions reflected the same intense focus that she had seen on the faces of soldiers before a mission. Even the youngest of the group would have made her think twice about challenging him. She returned her attention to the shimmering doorway when the Gateway opened in front of them.

11

On the other side of the shimmering portal, Avery could see Merrick crouched over Trudy. Addie was huddled next to them. Avery followed the four men through the opening, hoping the shooter couldn't see their shadows through the frosted glass in the front door.

While Core was barking a sharp warning to get down, Avery was silently cursing as she launched herself out of the path of the bullet. She hit the wall near the door. The bullet ripped through the door and created a hole in the wall across from her. There was no doubt in her mind that the shooter was a professional. She decided she would go with the more powerful of her two handguns. Pocketing the one she currently held in her hand, she reached behind her and pulled out the second gun as she rolled to crouch next to Trudy.

Merrick's eyes widened when he saw Avery. He turned and scowled at Core. Avery ignored them as she gently pressed her fingers against Trudy's forehead and looked down to where the other woman had been shot. Trudy's skin felt unnaturally cold and clammy, she was shivering, and a glazed look was beginning to cover her eyes. Trudy was going into shock.

"Who is she, and what are Teriff, Derik, and Hendrik doing here?" Merrick quietly grumbled.

"Teriff and Derik came to inform us that the council wants to meet with you tomorrow," Core snapped out. "Hendrik tagged along, and the female is Cosmos Raines' Head of Security and my bond mate."

"I am no one's mate," Avery snapped back. "Shit, Trudy. What the fuck are you doing here?"

Trudy turned her head with a moan. "Getting shot, what the hell does it look like?" she answered before her head sank back to the floor. "It hurts. I knew it would, but damn, no one said it would hurt this bad."

"She needs medical attention. We have to get her out of here," she said, looking up at Core.

Core held out the silver cylinder he had used to open the Gateway. "Avery, open the portal. Derik, take Avery and Trudy back to Baade," he instructed.

Derik nodded, moving around Trudy so he could gently lift her in his arms. They would have to move quickly once the Gateway opened. There was no telling where the shooter was and they already knew he could see them through the glass when the portal opened.

Avery hesitated. "Derik can carry Trudy through. I can help you here," she replied.

Core shook his head. "Go with Derik. He may need your assistance to save Trudy. Teriff has another Gateway device, and we can always notify RITA to send someone from Baade if we need to open another portal between our worlds," he replied.

Avery reluctantly nodded, knowing her first priority had to be Trudy. She looked over at Addie to see if the other woman was ready to move. Her heart clenched when she saw Merrick brushing the back of his fingers down Addie's cheek.

"Go with them," Merrick ordered in a husky tone.

Addie nodded, looking at Merrick with wide, frightened eyes as he moved down the hallway. Core followed Merrick, and Avery touched Addie's arm to get her attention. Startled, the younger woman jerked her head around to look at her. Avery signaled that Addie should follow her. Addie vigorously nodded.

Avery slid her gun into the pocket of her jacket and held up three fingers. She held the silver cylinder in her other hand. With a nod to Derik, she counted down, then pressed the button to activate the Gateway.

The moment the doorway shimmered into existence, Avery moved through the opening, followed closely by Derik with Trudy in his arms. Avery turned when she noticed that Addie had waited for Derik to go through first. She was motioning for Addie to follow when the cylinder in her hand suddenly shattered and the portal between the two worlds closed.

"Shit!" Avery cursed at the blank wall at the same time as she heard Derik's curse when Trudy began convulsing in his arms.

Core moved through the darkness parallel to Merrick, then paused and picked up a metallic casing from the ground. He held it up for Merrick to see. His cousin gave a sharp nod and pointed up into the trees.

Core looked up and saw a thick limb approximately fifteen feet above his head. He bent and jumped. His hands wrapped around the branch and he pulled himself up. Like the rest of his clan, he was an exceptional climber, as much at home in the trees as on the ground. In seconds, he had quickly scaled the tall fir tree. A break in the clouds overhead gave him a clear view of the ground below.

Core watched Merrick pause as the wind shifted. A faint scent on the breeze drifted up to him. One of their attackers had made the mistake of applying a flowery scent to his skin.

A movement forty yards to his right caught his attention. He uttered a short, musical whistle to alert Merrick. The whistle would be too high for the human to hear. Core narrowed his eyes when he saw two other humans. They had spread out.

He whistled again to warn Merrick. From his position in the tree, he could see one of the figures rise up and throw something toward the house before the man sank back down into the tall ferns. Core looked toward the second human as the man stood and began to move forward, some kind of gun in his hands.

Core silently dropped down to a lower branch as Merrick closed in on the first man. His teeth lengthened, and he crouched with one hand on the limb. Out of his peripheral vision he saw Merrick burst out of the darkness toward the human near him. Core released a terrifying growl of rage and jumped from the tree.

He landed on the ground behind the second man, grabbed the human by the back of his shirt, and lifted the slender man off his feet. He ripped the gun out of the man's hands, letting it fall to the ground as he pulled his knife from its sheath and drove it through the human's clothing into the tree trunk. Core left him hanging there. At least one of them would be alive to question at the end of this. He turned his attention to the third man.

Core almost laughed when the human's eyes widened in terror, and the man uttered a loud, terrified scream. He grinned, watching as the human stumbled backwards and fell to the ground. Stepping forward, he ground his booted heel into the human's weapon. The gun snapped under his weight.

"Please.... Don't hur... hurt us," the human whimpered.

"You're nothing but a boy," Core growled as he got a good look at him.

He turned his head to look at the other boy helplessly hanging on the tree. The boy had wet himself in his fright. Reaching out, he jerked the knife out of the tree. The boy crumpled to the ground and rolled into a shivering ball.

"We didn't mean anything!" the boy that Merrick had tackled cried out. "Please, it was just a joke! We were just joking!"

Core reached down and grabbed the two boys he had captured by the scruff of their necks, pulling them both to their feet. He pushed them toward Merrick. They fell to the ground in front of the tree.

Merrick released a low, menacing growl and crouched down in front of the crying boy. The other two were trying to curl up as small as they could get. Merrick rose to his feet and picked up one of their guns. It was nothing but a metal and plastic toy.

Merrick looked down at them as he demanded, "Who sent you?"

The crying boy wiped at his dirty face with one hand and held his right leg with his other. After so stupidly letting themselves be decoys, they should feel lucky they only had minor injuries.

Core scanned the area, looking for signs of anyone else. Teriff and Hendrick should be making their way back unless they had discovered something. He stared at a spot near the edge of the woods by the road, stiffening as he saw movement, but his warning died on his lips when he saw the shape more clearly as the large bird took flight.

"Some... guy... He was at the gas station. He said he had a friend staying here and wanted to play a trick on him. All... All we were supposed to do is fire some paintballs at the house. He gave us a hundred bucks and told us there was another hundred after we got done," the boy mumbled, his voice filled with tears.

Core turned back to Merrick when his cousin uttered a frustrated growl, lifted the toy guns in his hands, and broke them in two. He raised an eyebrow in warning when his cousin's teeth elongated. With a shrug, he turned his own sharp-toothed grin to the boys.

"Holy shit! We're gonna die," the boy who had wet his pants breathed in terror.

"You will if you remain here. Run home," Core warned in a low, harsh tone.

He and Merrick watched as the boys nodded at the same time. The two who were standing helped the third one up off the ground. In a hurried, clumsy gait, they stumbled through the ferns down to the road. Core turned and looked at Merrick with a frown.

"Why would the human killers use children?" he asked.

"Addie—they wanted a distraction to get to Addie," Merrick murmured, turning to give him a grim look.

Core looked back at the house. "She is safe," he said.

"Yes, but they don't know that," Merrick replied, turning toward the house. "Get Teriff and Hendrik, and meet me at the house."

Core nodded and turned on his heel. He took off across the grounds, keeping to the shadows. The hunt was not over.

12

Avery paced back and forth outside of the door to the medical room. Terra, Cosmos' wife/bond mate, was working to save Trudy. Avery glanced up when the door opened.

"Are they back?" she demanded.

Cosmos shook his head. His gaze moved to the door, and Avery pursed her lips.

"She's still in surgery, or whatever in the hell they do to people here," she said.

"Terra is an excellent healer, and the technology they have here is pretty exceptional. I can personally attest to that," he responded with a rueful smile.

"Once I know Trudy is out of danger, I'll return to CRI. If Merrick, Core, and the others don't find Markham, Wright, and Dolinski, I will," she stated, waving her hand in aggravation.

Cosmos reached out and grabbed her hand. She stiffened when he turned her clenched fist over, and pressed his thumb against the tips until she uncurled her fingers. He looked down at her palm, then locked gazes with her, his expression worried.

"Avery..." he started to say.

She shook her head. "It won't make a difference, Cosmos. I warned you, and I warned Core," she said, pulling her hand free.

Cosmos gave her an exasperated look. "Avery, this is something that you may not have much say about. This is deep. The science of it is mind boggling," he said.

She lifted her chin, and the expression in her eyes became cold. "I should have stayed focused. This...." She waved her hand and looked at the door. "This is what happens when you get distracted."

She stiffened when Cosmos wrapped his fingers around her forearms. Turning to look at him, she saw the anger in his eyes. He released her and stepped back with a shake of his head.

"This is what happens when bad people do bad things. It is not your fault, Avery. You know better than anyone else how much good we have done. We can't stop all the bad things that will happen. If anyone should feel responsible for what happened, it's me. It was my decision to get involved, and it was my invention that connected these two worlds," he said, turning away from her.

He stared through the glass at Terra as she worked to save Trudy's life. Avery reached out and squeezed his arm.

"You left your family's safety in my hands, Cosmos," she quietly reminded him. "Despite our best efforts, we are still only human. We can't protect everyone all the time."

He turned his head to look at her. "And I brought the forces of evil to them. I can't change the past—though I might try if I invent a time machine. We can't live in the past either, Avery. I know what happened to you. I've always known. I wouldn't have hired you otherwise." He turned to face her and grabbed her hand again. She looked down at her upturned palm. "I'm asking you to trust me on this. This connection is not something you can ignore—and you shouldn't. You should give Core a chance," he murmured.

Avery blinked and focused on the intricate design on her palm. She could feel Core. Even worlds away, she could feel him in her heart. Her mind and body craved the assurance that he was safe. Cosmos dropped her hand, and they turned when the door opened.

Terra gave them both a reassuring smile. "She will be fine. I would like her to stay in the medical unit for a few days so that I can monitor her. She lost a lot of blood and some of the damage was difficult to repair, but she is no longer in danger. If you would like to see her, you may go in. I do ask that you keep it short. I have given her medication to help her heal, and it will make her drowsy," she explained.

Avery looked at Cosmos. "You go in," he said. "I'll be here, and I'll check in on her later."

"Thank you," she murmured.

Terra stepped aside so that Avery could go into the medical unit. As she walked toward the door, Avery noticed the tender looks Terra and Cosmos exchanged as Cosmos wrapped his arm around Terra's waist.

Avery curled her fingers into a fist. This was not her—the tender expressions, the gentle caresses, the love—she wasn't even sure she was capable of such deep emotion.

She took a deep breath and focused on Trudy. This is where her comfort zone was—with her team. She walked across the room to the bed where Trudy was lying.

Her heart ached for the young woman lying on the silver sheets. A colorful band of lights suddenly scanned Trudy, and Avery turned slightly to look at Terra.

"It is a monitor. The computer will complete a diagnostic evaluation every five minutes for the first twenty-four hours or until all of her vital signs return to normal," Terra said from the door.

"No need to worry, Avery," RITA2 said, materializing in the chair on the other side of the bed. "I'll be here with Trudy until she is released."

"I love your new programming, RITA2," Trudy murmured. "Rose is going to be so jealous I saw it first."

"Wait until you see DAR. That man's program has me shorting out my circuits," RITA2 replied with an exaggerated wink while she fanned herself with her clipboard.

"Are you talking about me again, love?" DAR teased as he appeared next to RITA2 and dropped a kiss on her upturned lips.

Trudy giggled. "I see what you mean," she tiredly replied.

"DAR?" Avery asked with a raised eyebrow.

"Defense, Armament, and Response System at your service," DAR replied with a bow.

RITA2's eyes glowed—actually glowed—with humor. "I helped tweak his program at first, but the rest is all Prime computer code," she purred.

"Just what Earth and Baade need, their own set of horny AI computers messing with our worlds!" Avery dryly replied.

RITA2 rose from her chair and walked over to the bed. "You might learn a thing or two from us, Avery," she retorted.

"Ouch! Score one for the horny AI systems," Trudy muttered.

Avery bit her tongue to keep from making a sarcastic comment. She might not be as good as Trudy and Rose when it came to computer coding, but she was damn good at blowing things up. DAR must have recognized the glint in her eyes because he hurried over to RITA2 and wrapped his arm around her waist.

"Why don't we let Avery have a moment alone with Trudy, my love? There is a glitch in my program I want you to take a closer look at," DAR suggested.

"A glitch? Oh, that sounds like something that I have to take a *very* close look at," RITA2 breathed.

Avery watched as the AI couple shimmered and disappeared through the wall like twin apparitions oblivious to their surroundings. She blinked when she heard Trudy sigh wistfully.

"What's wrong?" Avery asked.

Trudy looked up at her. "I wish I could see his coding, too. I bet it is fabulous," she answered with another long sigh.

Avery shook her head. "You geeks are some of the weirdest individuals I've ever met," she replied.

~

Avery stepped out of the medical room twenty minutes later. She looked up and down the hallway for a moment before turning to the right and striding in a direction that she hoped would take her to an exit. She passed a series of windows that looked out over a beautiful garden. Even though it was dark outside, the moons and subtle lighting illuminated the area.

She spied a set of doors and headed for them. She was almost to the exit when she heard someone call her name. Turning, she waited for Cosmos.

"I'm sorry I missed seeing you leave the medical unit," he said.

She shrugged. "There is no need to apologize. I stayed longer than I intended. Trudy was telling me what she found out while I was gone. Have you heard from Core and the others?" she asked.

Cosmos nodded. "That is why I was pulled away. They've returned —with Weston Wright's body. Whoever he was with didn't want to give him the chance to talk to us," he explained.

Avery looked over Cosmos' shoulder as she sensed Core's presence, and locked eyes with him as he strode down the corridor toward them. It took more effort than it should have to pull her gaze away and look back at Cosmos.

"I'll return and locate Markham and Dolinski," she quietly said.

Cosmos turned around, saw Core, and then looked back at her. "Remember what I said, Avery, both about Core and what's happened. I want you to leave Markham and Dolinski to me. I'll personally handle this mission from here on out. That's an order, Avery. I know you can be like a starving wolf with a bone when you set your mind on something, but for once, I'd like to see you do something for yourself. I want you to take an extended vacation," he added.

Avery's eyes flashed with anger before she hid her emotions. She forced her pursed lips to relax. This was not the time to get into an argument. It wouldn't matter anyway. She had seen the same look of determination in Cosmos' eyes far too often to think he would budge from his decision.

"As you wish, Cosmos," she coolly replied.

Cosmos studied her face for a moment before he nodded in relief. "Terra says Trudy will be here for a few days. It will be nice to know you are here with her. I'll see you tomorrow," he said.

"Good night," Avery murmured.

She watched Cosmos turn and bow his head to Core before he

picked up speed and disappeared down the corridor. She turned on her heel and pushed through the door. The air outside was cool with a light breeze. It felt good against her heated skin.

She slid her hands into the pockets of her jacket, and reassured herself by curling her fingers around the pistol in one pocket and the silver cylinder of the Portal device in the other. It was the same device she had used to go from Cosmos' lab to Core's bedroom just a couple of days ago. As soon as it had become clear that Trudy was in good hands, Avery had borrowed one of the vehicles here and followed the alien version of GPS to Core's place to pick up the device, but by the time she was able to go back for Addie, RITA2 was informing her that there was no need.

Avery turned her head slightly when she heard the door behind her open. She slowly descended the steps to the path below. A moment later, the soft sound of Core's footsteps fell into rhythm with hers.

"What happened?" she asked, keeping her voice calm and her gaze focused on the path in front of her.

"It was Weston Wright, and we suspect Karl Markham. The man who shot Trudy also killed Wright," he said.

Avery nodded. "Cosmos said he suspects that Markham didn't want Wright sharing any information. From the little that I've been able to find out about Markham, it would fit his profile," she commented.

"They paid some youths to shoot colored balls at the house to draw us away. Wright was in the house, searching for Addie," he continued.

Avery paused and looked at him with a concerned expression. "Is she alright? I thought she was behind me, but a bullet shattered the cylinder you had given me. I could have immediately gone back for her if I had remembered to bring my Gateway device, but I didn't," she said with a frown. This was the second time she had failed Addie, and Avery fervently hoped she hadn't caused irreparable damage to the young woman.

"Addie was safe. She hid in a secret room they used for storage," he reassured her.

Avery stiffened when he reached out to enfold her in his arms. She wanted to push him away, but her body had other ideas. Instead of fighting, she stepped closer to him, slid her arms around his waist, and held him.

"No one was hurt?" she murmured against his shirt.

"Only the bad one. Merrick is quite upset. He was looking forward to killing the man," Core chuckled.

Avery turned her face into his chest and chuckled with him. They were a bloodthirsty lot. Weston Wright didn't know how lucky the end had turned out to be for him.

He wasn't that lucky. Merrick found him before Markham's bullet finished the job, he silently added.

"Markham is still out there—and so is Dolinski. They both need to be stopped," she murmured, tilting her head back to look up at him.

"They will be. Merrick will not rest until the humans have been found," Core replied.

Avery shook her head. "If anything, this should show how dangerous it is for your people to come to my world. This is something that we need to take care of," she insisted.

He slid his hands up from her waist and cupped her face, his expression hardening. She could hear his denial before he spoke. Turning her head, she pressed a kiss to the pattern on his palm.

"You are making me crazy," he groaned.

Her lips twitched. She looked up at him through her eyelashes, then wrapped her fingers around his wrist. Rising up on her toes, she pressed a hard kiss to his lips.

"Can we return to your home?" she murmured against his lips.

"Yes, I will borrow a transport," he replied.

"I'll wait for you out front," she said.

"I won't be long," he promised.

He reluctantly released her. Her fingers slid down his wrists and trailed along his palm to the tips of his fingers before he stepped away. She kept her mind focused on him and the memory of their touch.

In the darkness, the silver threads connecting their hands glowed again before vanishing. The strands reminded her of a spider's web. If you looked close enough, you'd swear that some magic had captured a thousand moons and stored them in the dew drops that clung to the web.

Her heart ached watching him walk back into the medical wing of the complex. He was a good man. Turning away, she looked up at the sky. The stars were different here. Even with two moons, she could see them so much clearer than back on Earth. She watched as a spaceship cut through the atmosphere.

This was a magical world where people lived by a different code. Humans weren't advanced enough for this world—not all of them. They would tear all of this down just like they fought to tear down their own if they had the chance.

She slowly lowered her head and looked around the garden, wondering, for just a moment, what it would be like to let go—to live a life where she could feel loved. Her hand slid down and she touched her stomach to remind herself why she couldn't.

"Dreams get you killed, Avery. Remember that," she whispered.

13

"This is Walt," a gruff voice answered.

"Have the helicopter ready," Karl ordered.

"Already is. Weston called earlier," Walt stated.

Karl's mouth tightened at his dead half-brother's name. He hadn't worked often with Weston, and if Karl hadn't brought him in on this case back when Avilov had hired him to deal with Tansy Bell... well, Karl wouldn't have had to shoot the weakling, would he? He'd be alive to annoy Karl another day.

"Destination?" Walt asked.

Karl's eyes narrowed. "Cancel the order. I need a jet instead," he replied.

"Destination?" Walt repeated, unperturbed by the sudden change in orders.

"Calais, Maine," he replied.

"It'll be ready at hanger C15," Walt replied.

Karl snapped the cell phone shut and placed it in the center console. His hands tightened on the steering wheel as he took a curve faster than was recommended. The BMW M760 sports car stayed true to the road like a champ.

He focused on the next step in his plan. There were more aliens than he'd expected—at least four of them. His eyes narrowed as he took another curve and the headlights of a car flashed by him. The women in Houston had been talking about someone getting close to an alien. Perhaps it was time to catch some new bait to use.

"Avery Lennox...." he murmured.

There was little information about her, but there was a photograph and he had a location—if she was still there. He reached for his phone again. He was surprised when an American voice answered his call.

"Name?"

Karl's brow creased as he frowned. He was normally patched through to a teen with a thick accent. Apparently he had gotten a receptionist, and she sounded like she was ten years old. For a second, he felt old.

"I need information on Avery Lennox, Head of Security for Cosmos Raines Industries," he replied.

There was a brief pause before the woman replied. "One hundred bitcoins."

Greedy little bitch, he thought before he answered.

"Agreed—if I get the information in one hour," he coolly responded.

"Same terms: all information transferred upon full payment," she said in a voice that sounded almost bored.

"Account name: Cohiba," he replied.

"You know smoking will kill you, right?" the woman-child dryly replied.

The connection ended before he could reply. He tossed the phone back into the console and accelerated. He hated dealing with hackers, but their expertise was sometimes needed. The last time he'd tried to access information on CRI and Avery Lennox himself, he had failed miserably, and promptly set up a job with this infamous 'Doughboy'. Karl sneered at the image that name evoked. The first job hadn't been for what he really wanted, though. Every contact needed to be tested, no matter how highly recommended they came. The hacker had passed with flying colors, and Karl had made a mental note to use him for the real thing if Merrick disappeared again. Karl had been so sure events at the cottage would go his way, but life had taught him to always have a surprise in his back pocket.

~

"Trudy is going to be fine, thank goodness," RITA said.

Rose almost dissolved in her chair. She laid her forehead on her folded arms and sniffed. Maria stood up from her position on the couch, came over, and hugged her.

"I remember what it was like when Rico was missing. I'm glad Trudy is okay," Maria quietly said.

Rose straightened and brushed her hands across her damp cheeks. Runt remained quiet. They had all been tense ever since they had received word that Trudy had been shot.

"Me too. Otherwise Avery would kick all of our asses," Rose joked in a trembling voice.

"Come on. Let's go get some hot chocolate and dessert. This calls for a celebration. Runt, you coming?" Maria asked.

Runt shook her head. "I'm good," she replied.

"Okay. If you need anything, give us a ring," Maria said.

Runt watched the two women walk out of the elegant office. The space felt more like a living room than an office, but it was the computer that made Runt feel at home. Her fingers moved to the mouse as the door closed behind the women, and she clicked open her previous screen. Her eyes widened when she felt her headphones buzz around her neck. The hacker she'd been monitoring had gotten a hit. She pulled them on.

Doughboy, aka the twenty-three-year-old who worked at a security firm in the Philippines, was a halfway decent hacker, moonlighting as a digital thief, fence, and illegal investigator. RITA had flagged Doughboy recently when he was contacted using a number she had identified as belonging to Weston Wright, but Runt had been following him long before she joined Cosmos' team. They'd had a few online run-ins a while ago, nothing major, but when he started getting a rep as the guy to go to if you needed a good fake id or info on someone, she'd started monitoring who he was working for and what he was doing for them.

Runt looked over her shoulder to make sure the door was closed all the way, then she looked back at the screen, swallowed, and intercepted the call. It was coming from the States.

"Name?" she answered.

There was a pause on the other end. For a second, she thought the guy was going to hang up. She wouldn't have blamed him. She obviously wasn't the person he'd been expecting.

"I need information on Avery Lennox, Head of Security for Cosmos Raines Industries," the man replied.

A shiver ran through Runt. This was Karl Markham. She would bet her computer on it. She recognized his voice from the video feeds —and the restaurant when he'd placed his order with the waitress. She bit her lip before responding.

"One hundred bitcoins," she stated, clenching her fingers around the mouse as she recorded their conversation.

She listened with growing apprehension as he agreed. She needed to warn Avery about Markham's investigation. The man had almost killed Trudy already; obviously he was dangerous.

Runt responded to Markham before disconnecting the call. She bowed her head and pursed her lips. She shouldn't have made that last comment. Who cared if the guy smoked? She hoped it did kill him!

"The call came from Oregon," RITA suddenly said.

Runt sat back in her seat and looked at the screen. In front of her was a map of the world with thousands of dots flickering.

She pulled a Ziploc bag out of her pocket, opened it, and set it on the desk next to her, absently pulling out a carrot stick to nibble on while she studied the monitor.

She had been looking into Markham for a while, but nothing so far had been helpful to pin down his home base. "He likes expensive cigars. That brand costs over eighteen grand a box. That will help us. Pull up the shipping logs of those suppliers," Runt instructed.

"Unless he is using the black-market or purchasing through an undisclosed retailer. I swear some of the older companies still use paper ledgers to do all their transactions. What do you want to do about Markham's request? Should I alert Avery?" RITA added.

Runt's fingers were already flying over the keyboard. She pulled up all the easy-to-find photos and information on Avery. Then she began creating a fictitious persona for her new boss.

"We give him want he wants—sort of. Does Avery look like she would carry a Coach purse?" Runt asked.

Runt looked up as RITA appeared, and reluctantly smiled when she noticed the AI had styled her hair and clothes remarkably like Avery's. Runt returned her attention to the computer screen.

"No, she wouldn't carry a purse," she muttered, answering her own question.

"Well, you don't want it to be too much like her. Let's say she attended Harvard Law School," RITA suggested, contributing the necessary documentation.

Runt's expression turned skeptical. "Law School? Are you kidding? She's the Chief of Security. She would have attended MIT or some fancy school like that, not Harvard," she scoffed.

"Mm, perhaps you're right. How about Harvard for Law and MIT for Computer Information and Cybersecurity? This way we have everything covered," RITA agreed, waving a hand at Runt's computer.

Runt giggled when the screen flickered and all the data changed. Within ten minutes, she had a full history created and spread throughout the web. Runt read through the official documents RITA had helped her create.

"I wish her life had been so simple," RITA said with a sigh. "You and Avery have a lot more in common than you realize, Amelia."

Runt shivered and pulled the sleeves of her tattered green sweater down until only the tips of her fingers were visible. She didn't reply. Her past was better kept hidden as well. When enough people wanted you dead, covering your tracks became pretty important.

Her palm tingled. She turned her hand over to look at the intricate design. It was growing more defined every day.

"RITA," she murmured.

"Yes, Amelia," RITA replied.

Runt looked up at the hologram with haunted eyes. "I don't want to be anyone's bond mate," she whispered.

RITA's softly glowing eyes gazed down at her compassionately. RITA was the closest thing to family that Runt had now. Sure Maria, Trudy, and Rose tried to make her feel like part of the team, but she couldn't relate to the other women. They teased each other and liked to go out. She preferred the quiet of the night, the hum of a computer, and the language of code.

Runt blinked in surprise when she felt her hair move. Her mouth dropped open when she realized that she could feel RITA's hand brushing the short, dark strands of her hair back from her cheek.

"FRED and I have been working on electrical pulses. It allows me to physically move things. Unfortunately, it is also very draining." RITA sighed with regret when her holographic form dimmed. "I don't think you'll have much choice, honey. These aliens have the whole mating thing down pat. It might be good for you, though. They are very protective, and they don't appear to have the incompatibility issues that humans have. If it is any consolation, you've got Derik tied up in complicated knots so tight, a veteran Navy man would be proud to have you on board his battleship."

"You're not helping," Runt scowled.

She wiggled her nose when RITA faded. She knew the AI was still there. RITA was always available if there was a device connected to the internet.

Runt looked back at the information she had provided. It was at least as thorough as the info Doughboy usually gave his clients. The guy was good, but not really better than the average self-taught programmer. She had slipped into his system through weak code that he should have cleaned up right away.

Markham on the other hand was a piece of work. He was smart. He didn't keep any electronics that weren't encrypted with some of the most current code out there. He also only had a few regulars. He wouldn't be using Doughboy again after she was done with the jerk.

Runt waited until Markham's bitcoins were ready for release.

Leaning forward, she clicked send and watched the exchange. Her fingers flew over the keyboard and a moment later the funds were transferred as a donation to a homeless shelter in New York. Their accountant would be having a heart attack when he or she came in the next morning.

Rising from her chair, she typed in a script that erased all trace of her transaction in Doughboy's account. Hopefully Markham wouldn't feel like going to the slums of the Philippines to find the hacker who had taken a nice chunk of change for fake information.

"Where are you going, love?" RITA asked.

Runt paused at the door to the office. "I wanted to let Rose and Maria know about Markham," she said.

"I'll ask my sis to pass on the information to Avery," RITA replied.

"Sounds good," Runt replied.

She pulled the door open and stepped out into the hall. After she let Rose and Maria know about the call, Runt would start planning her disappearance. She wasn't going to stick around to become some alien's property. She'd already dealt with one person who had thought of her that way.

14

Avery stood on the open deck that looked out over the water. They had returned to Core's home over an hour ago. It was late—or early depending on how you looked at the time. She had slipped outside while Core talked with Merrick about the council meeting tomorrow.

After everything that had happened in the last few months, she would be surprised if they didn't ban all Gateway technology. It should be obvious by now that humans were much more trouble than they were worth.

Absolutely not! We are warriors first! Core's thoughts came through loud and clear.

If Avery hadn't given up rolling her eyes when she was thirteen—well, except for the very rare occasion when she forgot—she would have done it now. Instead, she wrapped her arms around her waist and stared out over the moon-drenched water.

Our people need the Gateway, he continued.

Aren't you in a meeting to prepare for a meeting? Why are you talking to me? she silently retorted.

We are almost finished, he promised.

Take your time. I'm enjoying the beauty of the night. It isn't often that I get this type of solitude, she dryly thought back.

She could sense his concern before he withdrew—or at least pretended to withdraw. This form of communication was definitely different from what she was used to. Lifting a hand to her temple, she rubbed at the dull throb, then sighed when she felt Core's gentle touch. In seconds, the throbbing was gone.

What did you do? she asked.

I took your pain. Relax. I will be there in a few minutes, he tenderly replied.

Bring a glass of wine when you do, please, she responded.

His fading chuckle filled her with warmth. Once again he was gone—almost. She dropped her hand to the railing and leaned forward. A part of her wondered if their connection could stretch across the universe before she shook her head at the ridiculous idea.

"It truly is beautiful here," RITA2 said with a sigh.

Avery turned toward the AI. This time RITA2 was dressed in a silky nightgown with a matching robe that would have made a Victoria's Secret model drool. Avery raised an eyebrow.

"Have you been shopping?" she asked.

RITA2 twirled and grinned. "DAR's idea after our visit with Trudy," she replied.

Avery crossed her arms and gazed at RITA2 with a pointed look. "Is there a reason why you are here or are you so bored with advancing military defenses and intergalactic programming that you're selling lingerie now?" Avery retorted.

RITA2 chuckled. "First, Trudy is doing much, much better. The medical units on this world really are superior to those back on Earth," she said.

Avery waved her hand at the AI. "We haven't been gone from the medical center all that long and it was pretty obvious that Trudy was doing fine," she stated.

RITA2 hummed thoughtfully. "Well, I was just showing off a few new fashions to DAR to see if I could find the glitch he was talking about. Certain colors and transparencies of my nightgown caused an interesting spike in his coding. I'll have to ask RITA about it. I'm trying to decipher if it will cause long-term damage and how the vulnerability can be fixed," RITA2 explained.

Avery lifted a hand and pinched the bridge of her nose with her fingers. This was a case of definitely too much information, but RITA had never been programmed with Sex Education 101, and given that RITA2 was only a partial copy of RITA, it made sense that she wouldn't know how to analyze these kinds of things. Dropping her hand to her side, Avery looked at RITA2's perplexed expression and shook her head.

"DAR is horny. It sounds to me like you are giving that Prime computer system a digital version of an erection. Now, was there anything else you'd like to understand?" Avery asked.

"An.... Oh, that explains so much! Perhaps I should speak to Tilly. Yes, I think that is what I'll do. Tilly will know all about erections and horny men. She is constantly causing Angus' blood pressure to increase, even after all these years, and Cosmos can...." RITA2 said with growing enthusiasm and excitement.

"Enough! I don't want to think of Tilly and Angus that way, and I already feel like I need to scrub my brain without you adding Cosmos to the mix," Avery insisted with a shudder of distaste.

"You always were rather prudish when it came to sex, Avery. You should try shopping for something a little sexier than an oversized shirt with a football on it," RITA2 remarked.

Avery's fingers curled into her palm. "My night clothes are none of your concern, and neither is my sex life—which is anything *but* prudish, by the way," she growled.

"Yes, well, I'll have to monitor Core's blood pressure to see if it spikes," RITA2 responded with an indignant sniff. "I also came to tell you that RITA and Runt intercepted a phone call between Karl Markham and a hacker that Runt has been monitoring. He wanted information on you. Runt has thrown him off the trail for now, but you should be on your guard, Avery."

"Markham... What did he want to know?"

"He didn't ask for anything specific, just whatever could be found out about you. It isn't the first time. Before he hired help, RITA suspects he tried a few times to search himself, but she can't be completely certain because he always ended the search before she could pinpoint him. Clearly, he is aware that CRI was involved in shutting down Keiser and freeing Merrick," RITA2 added.

Avery nodded. "Thank you," she murmured.

"If there isn't anything else, I think it is time to test my theory with DAR," RITA2 replied.

Avery waved her hand. "That's all," she said.

RITA2 vanished as fast as she had originally appeared, and Avery tapped the railing impatiently. It was time to end this. If Markham was looking for her, maybe it was time he found her.

"I have brought your wine," Core said, stepping up behind her.

Avery brought her memories of the past two days to the surface, submerging all thoughts of Markham to a more private part of her mind. She turned around, and leaned back against the railing, smiling when she saw that Core had changed into a pair of loose fitting pants.

"I could get used to this," she murmured walking toward him.

She took the glass of wine from him and skimmed her free hand down along his bare chest, locking gazes him as her fingers trailed a fiery path to the edge of his pants. She took a sip from her wine, then leaned forward to smooth the tip of her cold tongue over his nipple. He swiftly inhaled a breath and rumbled a soft moan, standing still as she dipped her fingers into the wine glass and touched the droplet to the skin above his breast bone. She stroked his sides as she waited for the droplet to reach his stomach. Then she licked the trail it had left.

"*Ta me ja'te*, Avery," he murmured.

Avery closed her eyes when his words filtered through the translator Cosmos had implanted in her ear months ago, and she understood they meant *I love you.* A shaft of emotion pierced her. In response, she nipped his skin, causing a surprised curse to escape him.

He took the glass of wine from her, and placed it on the railing. She pressed tiny kisses up his chest until she reached his lips. Her hands moved down his stomach and beneath the waistband of his pants.

"I want you, Core," she murmured against his lips.

"Then you shall have me, *ku lei*," he replied, grabbing the hem of her oversized shirt, and pulling it over her head. She wasn't wearing anything beneath it.

"Ku lei," she whispered. "My beloved…" She gulped, knowing deep down the words were true. This relationship scared the shit out of her; yet at the same time, she felt stronger than ever.

Her breath hissed out in surprise when he suddenly bent and scooped her into his arms. She looped her arms around his neck. It still took her by surprise that he was strong enough to pick her up without a groan.

They didn't make it very far. He lowered her onto a nearby cushioned bench. She released him when he stepped back, and she hummed with pleasure when he pushed his pants down and kicked them to the side, her gaze fervently taking in his body.

She skimmed her hand up the side of his thigh, a smile teasing her lips when she saw his cock's reaction to her light touch. She locked eyes with him.

"Three days is not going to be long enough," he stated in a terse voice filled with emotion.

"No, it isn't," she admitted.

She wrapped her arms around his shoulders when he pressed her to lie flat against the bench and moved on top of her, lightly resting his weight against her length. His lips captured hers in a kiss that was a mixture of passion and desperation. Her legs rose and they came together, both determined to cling to the moment and forget about everything else. For the rest of the night, Avery reveled in this dream, and wished she could convince herself that it really didn't have to end.

15

Core watched Avery with amusement. She had an expression of bemused fascination on her face as she nodded in response to his little sister excitedly telling them about her incredible weekend.

Is she always this animated? Avery's sudden inquiry flashed through his mind and she glanced at his face before returning her attention back to Nadine.

She can be worse, he teased.

Nadine had appeared first thing this morning, unable to wait a moment longer to tell him about her weekend. He turned when the computer announced that his mother had also suddenly decided to visit.

I will return, he said.

Promise? she asked.

His heart warmed at the teasing in her voice. *Perhaps.*

Her silent chuckle echoed through his mind as he turned and hurried down to the lower level. He reached the level as the door opened and his mother stepped inside. His footsteps slowed when he saw the expectant expression on her face.

"Where is she?" Nadu demanded, eagerly looking around behind him.

Core shook his head. "How did you know she was here?" he replied.

Nadu smiled. "Word has spread all over the palace that there was another female from Tilly's world in the medical unit. Unmated warriors have lined up outside to see if she is a mate for them. During the council meeting, it was mentioned there was a second human female here as well. It did not take long for word to spread that she was seen leaving the palace with you. This is the one you have been talking about, yes?" she impatiently questioned.

His expression softened when he saw the excitement and relief in her eyes. He reached out and gently tucked her dark hair behind her ear. Her hands immediately lifted to smooth the wild tangle.

"Yes, Avery is here. Just how fast was Nadine piloting the glider?" he murmured.

Nadu shook her head. "I am lucky that my hair is not white. She has far too much of you and your father in her for a young maiden. Fortunately, there are no new dents for you to have to repair. Now, where is my new daughter?" she demanded with an impatient wave of her hand.

The smile on Core's lips disappeared. "I do not want to overwhelm her. Nadine has already slipped into the house by climbing the trees. Avery and I are still… working things out," he warned in a cautious tone.

"What do you mean… you are working things out? Did your father not have a talk with you? When a warrior finds his mate …." her voice died when he scowled at her.

"I do not need you to tell me about the Mating Rites. I am well informed about what happens," he growled.

Nadu leaned forward and brushed her hand affectionately across his cheek. "Your face is warm," she commented before patting it. "It is good to know that you did not listen to all of the nonsense about females not enjoying sex. The elders are either ignorant, stupid, or just miserable because they're not getting any. Your father is a very good lover. Have you used restraints? Tilly taught us that humans do not use them as frequently as Prime do, but when they are, there are many different ways mates on her world use them. Did you know that they can be used on males? I need to try them on your father when he returns. You should ask Avery if she would like to try a few other variations."

"I do not want the image of you and father together in my head," he said with a shudder. "Please promise me that you will not say anything about restraints to Avery."

He grimaced when he heard his pleading tone. How was it that it didn't matter how old he was, his mother still made him feel like he was an awkward teenage warrior? He cleared his throat and gave his mother a fierce glare that soon melted against her flushed cheeks and cheerful expression.

"I promise. Where is she?" Nadu asked.

They both turned when they heard Nadine's excited chatter coming closer. Core braced himself. This would be a true test—of his nerves. There was no doubt in his mind that Avery could handle both his sister and his mother. He'd watched her from a distance for months as she dealt with a wide variety of people. He just wasn't sure *he* could deal with it.

"And then there was a tall tree that I swear appeared out of nowhere and I had to turn the glider at the last second and we missed it by *this* much. It was so awesome! I heard Tink use that phrase. She says it means that something is very good. I had the best trip ever," Nadine said with a loud, contented sigh.

"It sounds like you had a very busy weekend," Avery replied.

Core studied Avery's expression as her amusement faded to cautious politeness when she saw his mother. What was worse—he could feel the wall in her mind rise to shut him out. Stepping forward, he grasped one of her hands in his and held it tightly as he turned to face his mother.

"Avery, I would like to introduce you to Nadu Ta'Duran, my mother," he quietly said.

"You warm my heart as much as you warm my son's—" Nadu started to say.

"—heart.... As much as she warms my heart as well," Core hastily interjected.

Avery turned to look at him with a raised eyebrow. "What did you think she was going to say?" she asked.

Core could feel his cheeks warm. He shot his sister a warning look when she giggled before he shrugged. It was impossible to lie to Avery.

"I'm not sure, but I fear it would be something that I would never live down," he sheepishly admitted.

Nadine giggled. "You've got a dirty mind, old man," she proclaimed with a regal wave of her hand.

Nadu looked at her daughter with a frown. "Was that a phrase in one of Tilly's educational films?" she asked.

Nadine shook her head. "No, that is what Tansy was saying to Lord Mak in the corridor when he could not take his eyes off of her. I asked Tink what it meant, and she said it means he is thinking things of a sexual nature—like Tansy warming his bed or doing warm things to his body," she answered, wiggling her nose in distaste. "I'm *never* going to do such things. I'm going to go to your planet and become a ticket-giver for your underground metal tubes and save individuals before they are hit by your travel machines. I'm gonna be a 'super-hero', and fight monsters, and become a pirate."

"Why would you become a pirate? They are horrible creatures who must wear a mask to cover their faces," Nadu demanded.

"I want to fight a giant and scale the cliffs and outsmart the evil prince. Why should men get to have all the fun? Tansy worked for her government. She was even gravely wounded. Avery, Core says that you fight bad men. One day, I can be like you," Nadine declared.

Core felt Avery's body stiffen and the smile that had formed on her lips faded slightly as her eyes became haunted, a wave of sadness sweeping over the mental wall between them. She reached out and carefully brushed a strand of Nadine's hair back from her cheek. The gentle gesture shook him to the center of his soul.

"You don't want to be like me, honey. You are a bright light in the world. People like me need people like you," Avery murmured.

"But... why? Why can't I be like you and Tansy?" Nadine protested.

"You have to grow up first," Core said. "I heard you did well piloting the glider."

Nadine's face lit up with her proud smile.

Several hours later, Avery stood holding a basket of fresh fruit and vegetables. They had been gifted to her as she and Core strolled through the village. She nodded and smiled at a young warrior who was looking at her with a mixture of curiosity, awe, and envy. More than once she felt an urge to pinch her arm to make sure she wasn't dreaming.

"They are happy to meet you. The Eastern Mountain clan has always lived in relative isolation, protected by the forest and the mists that surround us," Core explained as they walked along the path.

"Yet you travel to the main city on Baade," Avery murmured.

"Each clan has representation on the Council. Teriff rules over all the clans, but he is held accountable by the Council—or at least as much as they can contain him. Prime warriors are excellent fighters, but we do tend to have issues with authority, especially the clan leaders," he admitted with a wry grin.

She paused when a young girl who looked to be about six years old ran up to her with a handful of wildflowers, and offered her the colorful bouquet. Avery's throat tightened and she instinctively reached for them. Bending, she knelt until she was at eye level with the girl.

"Thank you. What is your name?" Avery quietly asked.

"Saylee," the little girl replied, beaming at her.

Avery carefully placed the flowers in the basket with her other gifts. "Thank you, Saylee," she murmured.

Saylee giggled and leaned forward to brush a kiss across her cheek. The display of affection took her by surprise. Her hand instinctively rose and touched the spot as Saylee turned and skipped away.

"She reminds me of Nadine when my sister was younger. My parents often told me that if I was ever blessed with a bond-mate and we had children, they hoped they would be like Nadine and me. It is said a union between a Prime warrior and a human tends to produce 'twins', so I imagine it is possible," he said with amusement.

Pain seared through Avery. She quickly blocked the emotion and stood up, her gaze following Saylee as the little girl ran back to her waiting parents.

"I have to go," she suddenly stated in a voice devoid of emotion.

"Where would you like to go next? There is a region to the north that I could show you…." he started to say before his voice faded.

Avery turned to look at him. "It is time for me to leave, Core. Our time is up," she quietly said, holding out the basket to him.

He reached out and took the basket from her with a confused frown. She knew he'd thought he could convince her to stay, and she did wish… but it was impossible. She didn't look away as his brief confusion changed to determination.

"Avery…. Let us return home," he said, reaching out to capture her hand.

She pulled back before he could, unwilling to touch him at the moment. Her emotions were too close to the surface for her to fight him and herself. She stiffened her shoulders and turned in the direction of his home. They walked in silence, nodding a greeting when one of the villagers called out to them.

Her gaze swept over the beautiful homes built among the majestic trees. She captured every detail and tucked them safely away into her memory. She had visited a magical world where love, hope, and peace were real—for a short time. She touched the petal of one of the flowers Saylee had given her. In a different life, such a reality might have been hers.

Her throat tightened as the lift took them up to the upper levels of Core's home. She stepped out into the living room, and walked into the kitchen. A minute later, she was carefully arranging the delicate flowers in a tall vase decorated with a swirl of vivid colors and dried flowers pressed within the glass.

"Why does life have to be so complicated?" she murmured. She continued before he could reply. "I promised myself three days because I knew if I stayed any longer, it would be impossible to leave."

"Life does not have to be complicated. You can stay, Avery," he quietly replied.

She felt the warmth of his body as he stepped up behind her. A shiver of need ran through her and she closed her eyes as it was followed by a shaft of anguish. Opening her eyes, she looked down at the delicate flowers. The stem of one of them was broken and it leaned sadly to one side. Her fingers gently tried to straighten the fragile stem, but of course the stem remained broken—like her.

"No, I can't," she said.

Her hand dropped to her side and she turned to look up at him. She opened her mind to him, allowing the memories she'd kept hidden to flow through to him. His face paled, but he didn't resist the visions she was sharing.

"The bullet that was meant to kill me went through my side and struck my hip. Fragments tore through my uterus. I was bleeding to death, and I didn't want to make the same mistake my parents did, Core. One way to prevent history from repeating itself was to make it impossible to conceive. My new handler told the doctors to remove my uterus rather than risk repairing it. It took 6 months to recover from my injuries, and then I spent years training to become the spy that my parents should have been. In another life, perhaps I could have been your bond mate, Core, but not in this one. My heart can belong to no one—not even you," she explained with a sad smile.

"We will make a new life, Avery. You are all that matters," he insisted.

She tenderly stroked his cheek. Her fingers traced a path down to the corner of his mouth, and she ran her thumb along his bottom lip. Rising up onto her toes, she pressed a light kiss to his lips.

"You are a good man, Core," she said.

She stepped around him. With her head held high, she walked out of the kitchen. *The Ice Queen indeed,* she scoffed at herself. Her heart hammered in her chest so hard she feared that it would burst. Pain swept through her. She let it flow. It was an emotion that she understood and had learned to handle.

A minute later, she entered the master bedroom. She had packed her bag earlier. Her hand slid into the pocket of her jacket and her fingers wrapped around the silver cylinder that would take her home. She pulled it free at the same time as she picked up her bag.

"This is not the end, Avery," Core quietly said behind her.

Avery turned to look at him. He stood in the entrance to the room, watching her, his determination unfazed. Her fingers tightened around the handle of her bag. She desperately wanted to drop the bag and throw herself into his arms. Her breath caught when he raised his palm to his lips and pressed a kiss to the mark that connected them.

Her lips parted in protest. Unfamiliar tears burned in her eyes. She shook her head even as she lifted the cylinder in her hand and activated the Gateway.

"Goodbye, Core," she whispered before she turned and forced herself to leave behind the heart that she had thought was frozen.

16

Core stood on the deck overlooking the river. His fingers tightened on the railing when he saw a dark shadow moving toward him along a nearby thick branch. He didn't want to talk to anyone at the moment.

"Go away, Merrick," Core ordered before his cousin had a chance to jump down onto the deck.

"RITA2 told me that Avery left," Merrick said, ignoring Core's order to leave.

Core scowled. "She needs to be disconnected," he snapped.

Merrick chuckled. "I'd be careful about what you say or DAR might take offense," he replied.

Core glanced at his cousin with an annoyed expression. He was about to give a sarcastic retort when he saw the look of concern on Merrick's face. Merrick turned to look out over the river.

"She's hurting and I don't know what to do," he suddenly admitted.

"Be there for her. Human women are very complex creatures. I believe your Avery is even more so.... She reminds me a lot of Lord Mak's mate. Perhaps you should speak to Tansy. She might be able to help you understand and give you guidance," Merrick suggested.

Core frowned. He didn't know why he hadn't thought about Tansy

Bell. She and Avery had many things in common. If anyone could help him understand what Avery was going through, it would be Tansy.

"Where is she?" he asked, turning to look at Merrick.

"Mak's island home. I would not go until tomorrow," Merrick replied.

Core nodded before he released a deep sigh. "How did the meeting with the Council go?" he asked.

Merrick muttered a few disgruntled words under his breath before he shrugged. "Pour me a drink and I will tell you. I swear it would have been easier just to remain isolated from the rest of the clans. The only reason I'm bothering to be a part of the Council is because they control who has access to the Gateway between our world and Earth," he muttered.

Core started to turn away. "The Gateway device we had was destroyed. We need another if I am to travel after Avery," he said.

Merrick looked at him with a serious expression. "All access between the worlds has to be preapproved and strict regulations have been added. The Council does not want a repeat of what happened to me. The human President has also informed Cosmos that he does not want any aliens running around without prior notification. Even RITA2 has been barred from interfering or giving unauthorized access to the Gateway. Any violations will result in RITA2's quarantine," he explained.

A soft curse escaped Core. His stomach tightened at the thought of not being able to go after Avery. He was already feeling the effect of their separation.

"I have to be granted permission, Merrick. You have to help me," he said, looking at his cousin.

Merrick flashed him a grin. "I'm a member of the Council now. Of course I'll help you," he replied.

A reluctant smile curved Core's lips. "The Council has no idea of what they've done by letting you on the panel, do they?" he remarked.

Merrick slapped him on the shoulder, causing him to wince. His cousin's strength was returning. He rubbed the offended area.

"No, they don't. Teriff thought it was time for some new blood on the Council. I'm sure it has nothing to do with the fact that Derik's bond mate is almost of age," Merrick replied with a sharp-toothed grin.

Core turned and walked back inside, listening as Merrick talked about the Council members from the Northern, Southern, and Western Clans. He was pouring them both a drink when Merrick got to the part where the Council had discussed the Juangans, a vicious, pirating, reptilian-like species, who were ramping up their attacks on military and merchant shipping alike.

"If the Juangans are not contained soon, it may well be war," Merrick was saying.

Calais, Maine:

Avery stood frozen on the other side of the Gateway in Cosmos' lab, letting her body tremble with the aching emotions engulfing her.

She forced her feet to move through the security measures. The sound of her boots against the concrete echoed in the cavernous room. Once through, she gripped the railing as she climbed the metal staircase to the upper level.

When she reached the top, she looked back at the doorway. Nothing but concrete showed now. Avery blinked away the tears blurring her vision. Lifting her head, she turned her back on what she had left behind and walked along the landing to Cosmos' desk.

"Block it, Avery," she murmured to herself.

She carefully placed the silver cylinder on the note that Cosmos had left her. For a second, the impulse to grab the cylinder and open the Gateway almost overwhelmed her.

She closed her eyes. Images of Core rose in her mind's eye. A bittersweet smile curved her lips as she remembered his teasing, their laughter, and his touch. She forced her eyes open when she felt her phone vibrating in her pocket. Drawing in a deep breath, she fished her cell phone out. Glancing at the number, she swiped her finger across the screen.

"How can I help you, Secretary Albertson?" she answered.

"I've been calling. Where have you been?" Richmond demanded.

Avery's eyes narrowed at his sharp tone. "I don't work for you, sir. Therefore, my other commitments took priority," she replied in a cool tone.

"...Yes... of course. Are you in Houston?" he asked.

"Not at the moment. I will be returning to Houston this evening," she replied, placing her bag on the desk before she rubbed at the ache forming between her eyes.

"I would like to meet with you. Is it possible for you to come to my home in Virginia?" he inquired.

Avery closed her eyes irritably. This was one of the reasons her days of working for the government were long past.

"I can meet you in Washington," she countered.

He was silent for a moment before she heard him exhale. The spoiled politician would just have to deal with the inconvenience. It wasn't her job to make him happy. In fact, at the moment, she could happily tell him to go fuck off. She wanted to get back to her apartment, take a hot shower, and get her emotions back under control before she dealt with anyone. She impatiently waited for his answer.

"In Washington then. When will you be here?" he demanded in a gruff tone.

"I'll take a flight this afternoon. I can meet you later this evening or sometime tomorrow," she dispassionately offered.

"Tonight, ten o'clock at the Jefferson Memorial," he said.

"I'll see you at ten o'clock," she agreed, "Can I inquire about the purpose of this meeting?"

"It's a matter of national security. I'll brief you when we meet this evening. Don't be late," he replied in a terse tone before he disconnected the call.

Avery stared at her cell phone. Her gut twisted. The hand that had been rubbing the throbbing spot between her eyes moved to her stomach. She didn't know if her pain was a manifestation of her feelings for Core or nerves about the upcoming meeting, but this was certainly not the time to get soft.

Avery looked down at her palm. The intricate mark pulsed with the same beat as her heart. Her fingers curled into a tight fist. The longing to go to him was threatening to break through the walls she had built.

She looked up at the ceiling. This was what she imagined withdrawal from drugs would feel like. She needed to see him, touch him, hear his voice.

Her gaze turned to the silver cylinder. She had to get out of here. Her original plan had been to take a shower, catch up on her emails, and check in with Rose and Maria before calling for the corporate jet to return her to Houston. Now she would only be doing the last part.

Pushing the number for the corporate pilot that was on standby for her, she picked up her bag and began walking toward the exit of the lab. Each step away from the Gateway device and her only hope of seeing Core again was agonizing. The deep voice on the other end of the phone pulled her back to the present.

"I'll be there in an hour. File a flight plan to Washington, DC. I'll also need a car and driver," she stated.

"Yes, Ms. Lennox. The jet will be fueled and ready to go when you arrive," Rex cheerfully assured her.

"Thank you," she replied, ending the call.

"You know, Cosmos might get a little upset if you *accidentally* forget to return a Gateway device, but I'll never tell him," RITA replied, suddenly appearing to walk beside her.

"I want to be alone, RITA," Avery gritted through clenched teeth.

"Avery…." RITA started to say.

Avery turned on the AI system. Her eyes flashed with pain, grief, and fury. She would not have her life controlled by anyone—not even an advanced computer system.

"Terminate this conversation immediately, RITA, or I will personally speak with Cosmos about your interference," Avery warned.

"As you wish, Avery," RITA quietly replied.

RITA faded, and for a moment Avery looked through the clear

doors to the main part of the building, then she struck her fist against the clear material. The sound of the case of her cell phone striking the material reminded her that she was still holding it.

Blinded by tears, she pocketed her phone and activated the door leading out to the hallway. Her speed picked up and soon she was running down the stairs instead of taking the elevator to the parking garage under the warehouse.

She strode across the dimly lit parking lot to the Tesla. The doors unlocked as she approached. She opened the passenger door and tossed her bag inside, then slammed the door shut and walked around the car. Grief hit her hard as she pulled the driver's door open. Lowering her head, she did something she hadn't done since she was a child—she let the tears fall without trying to stop them.

Karl impatiently tapped his fingers on the steering wheel of the car that he'd been living in the last three days. He ran his hand along his jaw. The rough stubble irritated him almost as much as the grainy feel of his eyes from lack of sleep.

He knew Avery Lennox had to be still in the building. A soft curse escaped him when he felt his full bladder protest. He was about to push open his door when a movement from across the street caught his attention. A sleek red Tesla pulled out of the parking area under the warehouse. In the driver's seat was Avery Lennox. She paused and looked both ways before she pulled out onto the street.

His bladder would have to wait. Pressing the ignition button, he pulled out behind the Tesla. He'd spent a lot of time planning what he would do next. He'd also read over the report on Avery Lennox.

There hadn't been much about her. Lennox was clearly well versed in keeping her life private. The limited information about her hadn't been worth the high cost—but, he knew that she had a vulnerability.

Avery Lennox cared about people. That information hadn't come from the little thief he'd paid a fortune to, it had come from his own sleuthing. He had combined the report he'd received with other facts from his contacts in the government, as well as public news articles, and he'd discovered that Avery Lennox's life was dedicated to helping and protecting people.

The death of Adam Raines had hit her hard. His new dossier contained a picture of her, composed and protective as she stood behind Cosmos and Ava Raines at the cemetery. He'd studied that image of her and noted her terse remark to the reporter who had covered the funeral. *'Those responsible for Adam Raines' death will be brought to justice—one way or another.'*

Avery Lennox didn't get mad, she got what she wanted. His informant in the government had said the same thing. Richmond Albertson, the Secretary of State, had been very candid with him, though he hadn't exactly been a fount of *specific* information as he warned Karl that Avery was more dangerous than she appeared to be. All Albertson knew was that Lennox was smart, seemed to know things she shouldn't, and that she worked for Cosmos Raines—who also wasn't all he appeared to be. Karl didn't need Albertson to tell him that, and it was obvious Albertson knew nothing about what Raines had been up to. If Raines was palling around with aliens, what else was he capable of? Avery Lennox would know the answer to that question, and now that she was back, it was time to schedule a meeting before she disappeared again.

He looked down at his phone when it vibrated. Seeing the caller's name, he reached out and picked up the phone. Pressing the answer icon, he waited without speaking.

"She's meeting me at the Jefferson Memorial tonight at ten o'clock," the voice on the other end stated.

"Meet her alone. Leave your security personnel behind," he responded. There was silence on the other end. A smile curved his lips when the silence grew longer. He knew what Albertson was thinking. "You are still useful to me, Richmond."

"I'll meet her alone," Richmond hesitantly agreed, then he took a breath as if to say something, but apparently lost his nerve.

"What is it?" Karl finally demanded, allowing a touch of his irritation to seep into his voice.

"She'll know I set her up," Richmond replied in a slightly desperate tone.

His eyes narrowed on the car in front of him. "There is no need to worry about Avery Lennox, Mr. Secretary. I'll take care of everything," he replied before ending the call.

His gaze narrowed on the red Tesla pulling farther ahead of him. He knew where she was going so he didn't need to follow her now. Pressing the call button on his phone, he quickly made arrangements for his own flight to Washington, DC.

17

The sound of a door slamming against the wall ricocheted through the long corridor outside the Council chambers. The fury on Core's face caused several warriors standing outside the room to move out of his way very quickly. They warily watched him stalk past them. His white-knuckled grip on the sword at his side gave them ample reason to worry.

"Core..." Merrick called out behind him.

He ignored his cousin. Pain, desperation and rage swept through him. He was very close to losing what little control he still had after the hour-long argument with the Council. He heard a pair of booted feet following him.

He turned and pushed open the doors leading out to the central gardens. Stepping outside, he crossed the veranda and descended the steps. He needed a moment alone.

"Core!"

This time it was Teriff's voice that called out to him. He slowed his footsteps and came to a halt. He rolled his shoulders to ease the tension as he waited for Merrick and Teriff to catch up with him.

Turning, he scowled at his cousin when Merrick took his left side while Teriff took his right. Merrick looked down at Core's fingers with a pointed glance. He grimaced and loosened his grip on the hilt of his sword. His rage was not directed at them, but at the other men who were currently debating his and Avery's future. He flexed his fingers and forced himself to relax.

"How much longer must they contemplate whether it is a good idea to continue using the Gateway device? It's been almost two weeks," Core growled under his breath.

"I know," Merrick replied with a sympathetic look.

"If the Council tries to deny the use of the Gateway, there will be a planet-wide revolt and they know that," Teriff said. "Too many warriors—especially from the different clans—now know there is a world where there are many potential bond mates. You know as well as we do that the clans will not allow this opportunity to be denied without a fight. You have Merrick's and my vote."

Core lowered his head and took in a deep, calming breath. The unease inside him was growing. He knew a portion of it had to do with his separation from Avery, but there was something else as well.

"They know she is my bond mate. They know what will happen if they continue to keep us apart," he said. He lifted his head and looked at Teriff. "She must know by now how powerful our connection is—and how difficult it will be for us to be separated."

"The Council promised to vote this evening," Teriff replied. "If they refuse, I will make the decision. I prefer not to, because I can't kill the opposing members of the council and they will make sure there are consequences for overriding them. There are some days that I miss the old ways when we just battled it out until the last warrior was standing," Teriff stated with a sardonic grin.

Core nodded, feeling hope for the first time in more than two weeks of meetings with the Council. He turned his head and nodded to Merrick when he felt his cousin squeeze his arm in support.

"You'll bring her back here," Merrick said with a confident nod, "or I'll help Teriff battle the others."

Core dryly chuckled. "I would help you," he replied.

***

Remote island off of the South Atlantic Ocean:

Avery stared out of the window of her prison cell. The miniature fortress sat on the edge of a cliff. She could see a line of jagged rocks rising from the churning ocean below. The artificially heated room was evidence that outside temperatures were frigid. There was no escaping—at least not from this room. The walls were thick stone, and the windows had reinforced polycarbonate on the inside of the double pane. Even if she could break through the glass, she would face certain death by either falling to the rocks below or plummeting into the freezing, turbulent waters.

It'd been almost ten full days since she'd woken here. Over the course of the last seven evenings, all she'd learned was that she was being held on a remote island somewhere in the Southern Hemisphere.

Avery turned and looked at the door to the elegant accommodations. The interior door was a grate of thick iron bars. The outer door was beautifully carved wood. No one would know from the outside corridor that this room was a prison cell.

Avery smoothed her beautiful red evening gown. Markham was a misogynist with delusions of grandeur, and he expected her to dress in the designer gowns for their formal evening meals.

Once every evening she was escorted out of the cell so that she could join her captor for dinner. She had learned the first night that her attendance was not optional. When she had tried to resist, she was chained—and beaten.

She had to give Markham credit. He was good at torture. He'd kept the bruising to a minimum while making sure that she felt what he'd done every time she moved. After the third day, she realized that resisting didn't serve her best interests. There'd be no way to escape if she was physically incapable of moving.

Her lips tightened when she heard the key in the door. She would entertain the bastard—right up until she slid a knife between his ribs. Avery smiled slightly at her bloodthirsty thoughts. She was sure Markham wouldn't find them nearly as funny as she did.

The bloodstains will go well with this gown's color, she thought with morbid amusement.

Her smile faded when her gaze locked on the pleased look on Markham's face. The bastard was definitely up to something.

"Time for dinner," he stated, unlocking her cell door.

She walked with her head held high. No matter what happened, she would never give this asshole the satisfaction of feeling completely in control. She started to step through the doorway when she felt his hand on her arm. Her body stiffened at his touch and she turned her head to glare at him.

"You look very lovely tonight, Ms. Lennox," he murmured.

Her lips pursed together. Her suspicions bloomed faster than the finale at a Fourth of July firework show. There was something different about him tonight—he almost exuded a sense of anticipation.

"I thought tonight we would dine in my personal study," he commented.

Avery fell in step beside him as he guided her down the corridor. Today, six men kept pace with them. She paused when they proceeded past the grand staircase that led down to the lower level, and she frowned when she saw another six men carrying large containers into the foyer. One man stepped forward and opened one of the long black crates. She immediately recognized the wide assortment of munitions inside. The man looked up at her. His eyes flashed to Markham before he returned his attention to the crate and closed the lid.

"This way," Markham ordered.

Avery started walking again when he firmly tugged on her arm. They strolled down the corridor to the very end where a pair of oversized double doors stood open. Through the doorway, Avery could see a large, heavily carved desk made of dark wood—perhaps mahogany. Above it was a painting of a woman who appeared to be in her early sixties. The woman would have been timeless if not for her clothing and her gun. On either side of her were the sprawled bodies of a male lion and a lioness.

Avery stepped inside and took a moment to scan the room. In front of the massive stone fireplace and its cheery fire was a small dining table set for two. The room took up the entire west side of the upper floor of the fortress. On each side of the fireplace stood a stag, the pair forever frozen in mid flight.

The room was filled with trophies of big and small game alike. Distaste filled her when she saw the number of endangered animals among the mounts. Her eyes widened when she saw a perfect replica of the woman, the lion, and the lioness in one large clear display case.

She walked over to the case to examine it. The three were posed as if they were waiting for the artist to finish his painting. Her eyes moved from the display case to the painting and back again. With a horrified fascination, she realized that the body of the woman in the case was as real as the two lions she had killed. A shudder ran through her.

"She was a fascinating woman," Markham remarked.

Avery schooled her features to hide her growing unease, and looked up at Markham when he came to stand beside her. He held out a glass of red wine. Her gaze moved to the glass and she reluctantly took the goblet from his hand, then turned back to the gruesome display.

"Who was she?" she inquired.

"Priscilla Housing—my mother. Weston's too, of course," he replied.

She watched as Markham raised his glass in a toast to the dead woman before he took a sip. He turned to look down at Avery, his lips curved in a smile that did not reach his dark eyes.

"She was a true sadistic bitch," he added.

When he began walking along the line of cases that filled more than half the room, Avery followed him, all of her instincts on Code Red alert.

"Why...? Why keep her like this?" she asked.

Markham looked at her and shrugged. "She was the very essence of Diana, Goddess of the Hunt. She was the predator who never missed her target. When her reign ended, it seemed only fitting that she live on like the prey she immortalized," he explained.

...*Wow,* Avery thought. This man redefined 'major mommy issues'.

Avery looked back at the display case with a grimace. "The painting of her wasn't enough?" she asked.

Markham turned to face her. There was no expression on his face, but his eyes—there was something just not right in his eyes.

"A painting is two dimensional. Priscilla Housing was anything but a two-dimensional woman. She hunted and killed this lion and lioness, but only after she had killed the rest of the pride," he said reverently. "The true joy comes not in the kill, but in the hunt, Ms. Lennox. When you triumph over a predator as cunning as yourself, it is only right that you preserve your victory as a trophy," he stated.

A disturbing understanding swept through her. "You... killed her. You murdered your mother?" she whispered.

Markham shook his head. "No, I hunted her... and proved I was the top predator," he replied.

Avery stood frozen as Markham paused by several empty display cases. Her eyes followed the movement of his hand as he removed a handkerchief from his pocket and wiped at an imaginary smudge on the clear surface. The plaque on the display read:

Exhibit One: Alien Male
And Human Female Companion

Markham pocketed the small, rectangular cloth and turned to gaze back at her. Nausea rose in her throat.

"Dinner is served," he announced.

She stepped to the side as he walked by her, unable to do anything for a moment but stare at Markham. He waited by her chair as the servant placed their meal on the table, his eyes locked on her face. Avery knew from his satisfied expression that she hadn't been successful at hiding her horror and revulsion.

She lifted her chin. She had to get out of here. There was no way in hell that she was going to end up as an exhibit in this bastard's House of Horrors! Her gaze drifted over Priscilla Housing's body as she walked past her. Fear turned into a cold, determined rage. She lifted the glass of wine to her lips and took a sip before she placed it on the table by her dinner and gracefully sank into the chair that Markham had pulled out for her.

He walked around the table and sat down in his seat. She waited for him to pick up his spoon before she reached for hers. Avery slowly stirred the chilled Green Tomato and Crabmeat soup. Her spoon paused when he spoke again.

"So, tell me everything you know about your alien, Ms. Lennox," he calmly ordered.

18

Cosmos Raines Industry's Houston Headquarters:

Core glared at RITA before turning his aggravation on Cosmos. He couldn't beat the shit out of an AI system. Instead, he took his anger and frustration out on the human who was warily watching him.

"When is the last time you heard from her?" he demanded.

"She received a phone call from Secretary Albertson the day she returned," RITA interjected. "And then she flew to Washington, D.C. Avery's driver said he dropped her off near the Jefferson Memorial. That was the last time he saw her."

"We've been going through video from the area's surveillance cameras," Cosmos said, his frustration palpable. "It's as if she vanished into thin air. Our delayed return to Earth didn't help. I thought the Council was never going to get off their asses and make a decision."

"Father finally threatened to replace the lot of them—except Merrick, of course—if they didn't make a decision he approved of," Terra murmured.

"You didn't tell me that," Cosmos curiously commented.

Terra reached out and ran her fingers along his cheek. "You were with Trudy," she answered.

Core could see they were privately sharing more with each other. He turned away and walked over to the window. After RITA2 had opened the portal here and RITA told them Avery was not here, he and Cosmos had asked why they had not been informed earlier that Avery was missing. She had replied that no one had realized it was a problem—until now.

"Tell me again what the driver said," Core demanded.

"That Avery instructed him to return to Houston," RITA answered. "She said that she would be doing some work from the Washington, D.C. townhouse and would let Robert know when she returned to Houston. He said that she appeared distracted when he picked her up at the townhouse, but that was not unusual. She intended to take a taxi when she was ready to return after her appointment. There are no records of her ever doing that. Rose and Maria thought Avery had extended her vacation. It was only when I tried to pinpoint her location that I realized her phone was off," RITA explained with an apologetic tone.

"Surely the fact that she hadn't made any phone calls or used her computer should have been some kind of indication!" Cosmos growled, running his fingers through his hair.

"It isn't unusual for Avery to go off the grid, Cosmos," Rose replied.

Maria nodded. "Avery knows better than anyone that electronic devices can be traced or tapped. I know she had some reservations about Albertson. She requested that we do a forensic audit of his finances. We already have the accounting team on that," she added.

"His money trail is quite intricate," RITA replied.

"So at this point all we know is that Avery's last known contact was with Richmond Albertson," Cosmos stated.

"He's working with Karl Markham," a soft voice said.

Core turned to look at the quiet, dark-haired woman who looked far too young to be a part of the team. She had slipped into the room behind the other two women when Cosmos had called this meeting. She was wearing an oversized coat that made her look even smaller than she was. She had curled up on the couch with a small laptop and been silent until now.

"How do you know, Amelia?" Cosmos asked.

"He's been sending payments to one of Markham's offshore accounts. I've been focusing on Markham. He contacted a hacker to get info on Avery. I intercepted the job, then RITA and I gave Markham a bunch of crap mixed with known facts, but what's important is he gave me the name of the account he'd set up with the hacker, which eventually led me to one of Albertson's foreign bank accounts," Runt explained.

Core looked at Cosmos. He was about to ask Cosmos where he could find this Albertson when he noticed that everyone in the room was looking at the young woman with their mouths hanging open. He was about to ask what was wrong when Cosmos grinned at the small woman and said, "I don't think I've ever heard you say so much at one time." Cosmos chuckled with a shake of his head.

The woman scowled at him. "Whatever," she muttered with a shrug and looked back down at the computer in her lap.

Once again, Core was about to say something, but this time Cosmos' cell phone rang. Cosmos pulled his cell phone out of his pocket and looked at it. His frown melted into an expression of relief, and he grinned at Core.

"It's Avery," he said, answering the call and lifting the phone to his ear.

In an instant, the relief disappeared from Cosmos' expression, his face hardened, and his body tensed. Core stepped closer.

"Where is she?" Cosmos demanded in a harsh tone.

"It's Karl Markham," Runt said at the same time as RITA did.

Anger burned in the pit of Core's stomach. Cosmos locked eyes with Core, then lowered the phone and pressed a button. The man's grating voice filled the room.

"Do you have the ability to contact one of your aliens, Mr. Raines?" Markham asked.

"Where is Avery, human?" Core demanded.

There was a brief silence before a low, menacing chuckle came over the phone. "I will send a vehicle for you. Come alone and unarmed. If you break either of those conditions, I'm afraid I will have to terminate Ms. Lennox with a very painful death," Markham instructed.

"Put Avery on the phone," Cosmos demanded.

Markham laughed again. "I'm afraid Ms. Lennox isn't available to talk at the moment. She is currently… asleep," he said.

"How do we know you even have her, then?" Cosmos said, looking over at where Rose and Maria were frantically working with RITA to pinpoint the location of the call.

"I could send you a piece of her to assuage your doubts, Mr. Raines. Perhaps the hand with the markings on it would convince you," Markham coolly suggested.

"Touch her and I will enjoy ripping you apart," Core growled.

"The car will be in front of your building in one hour," Markham replied with another chuckle before he ended the call.

"Son-of-a-bitch," Rose cursed, looking up at Cosmos and shaking her head.

"He removed the tracking software in Avery's phone and has a scrambler on the signal," RITA said. "Given enough time, I might be able to narrow down his location."

"He's on an island in the South Atlantic," Runt said, looking up at them.

Cosmos frowned. "How do you know?" he asked.

Runt raised a delicate eyebrow. "He is using the same phone he used to contact the hacker. I uploaded a cookie so I could track when and where he made a call. There aren't a lot of options in his location for connectivity. He was using a satellite that belongs to the CRI Communications Division," she expanded.

"Avery was right. You are one of the best," Cosmos said with a nod of approval.

"Using the information Amelia has given us, I believe I have located Markham," RITA said.

A three-dimensional hologram of an island appeared in the center of the conference room table. Core stepped forward to get a better look. On a cliff along the northernmost end was a man-made structure.

"I'm trying to access the security systems, but am unable to do so. It appears he has a self-contained system," RITA said.

"What are we going to do?" Rose quietly asked.

"I am going to go after her—and kill Markham and anyone else who gets in my way," Core replied.

"I have a few things for you," Cosmos said, entering the room.

Core's gaze narrowed on the small black bag in Cosmos' hand. Terra walked beside him with a set of clothing that had clearly come from Baade. He frowned when Cosmos placed the bag on the table of the conference room and began to unpack the items inside.

"Markham said no weapons," Core replied.

Cosmos shot him a grin. "Yes, well, we'll call these tools," he quipped.

Terra placed a Prime warrior's vest and belt on the table. Next she set down a pair of boots that seemed identical to the ones he was wearing. She gave him a reassuring smile.

"Cosmos and I have been working on a number of innovations using a blend of our technology and his," she said.

"The buttons of the vest are filled with explosives," Terra instructed. "Twist to the left, then to the right and it will activate the chemicals inside. You will have thirty seconds before it explodes. It will have a blast radius of several yards.

"The buckles on the sides of the vest contain wire the width of spider's silk. It can hold up to 520,000 pounds per square inch. You'll have a total of five hundred feet of rope if you connect the buckles together. If you attach the end of the thread to your right boot and pull it taut, it will automatically lift you.

"Your wrist band has three small grappling hooks. Attach one of the wires to it and press this hidden button to launch the hooks. In a pinch, it can also be used as a weapon.

"Along the inside seams of your boots are three arrows. The outside seams pull off to form a bow. All these items are made of organic materials and will not register on a metal detector. It is highly unlikely that the items could be discerned even under close visual scrutiny. I've added two daggers along the inseams of the vest as well. The right heel contains a few small devices to record visual content. I have contacts for you to wear to access them," Terra explained, showing him each item.

Core looked at Cosmos as he held up a small, decorative patch with the CRI emblem on it. "I've been playing with some of your technology," Cosmos said, then he placed the patch on his own shirt. A surprised curse slipped from Core's lips when Cosmos held his hand over the patch—and disappeared. Core stepped forward and reached out. He was surprised again when he felt Cosmos' arm.

Cosmos dropped his hand and he reappeared, his eyes twinkling with satisfaction as he handed the patch to Terra. She affixed it to the front of the vest.

"We have technology like that?" Core asked.

"We do now," Terra replied.

Fascinated, Core picked up the belt. This one was devoid of the customary utility compartments. Terra took it from him and stepped back.

"If you pull the belt taut, you'll see that it changes into more than your typical belt. The end has two spring loaded blades which form a sword," she said with a smile.

"The hardest thing to conceal was a medical kit. We don't know what shape Avery will be in," Cosmos quietly added.

Terra nodded. "We both consider Prime technology far superior, but concealing a portable emergency medical unit would be impossible," she said.

"So, we compromised," Cosmos explained.

Terra pulled a small injector out of her pocket and stepped close to him. She motioned for him to roll up his sleeve, then gently grasped his arm and placed the tip against his skin. He heard the soft sound of the medical injector and felt a brief sting before she stepped back.

"I've developed a prototype healing agent. The injection I gave you is filled with nanobots designed to seek out and repair damage. They will activate the moment they detect any injuries or infection. Once they do, they will continue to replicate for forty-eight hours before they dissolve. You can share them with Avery if you bite her and they enter directly into her bloodstream. The amount of damage they can heal is limited, but we hope it will be enough to stave off a medical emergency until we can get you both off of that island," she instructed.

"No one comes until I have her secure," Core warned.

Cosmos nodded. "I put a miniature emergency beacon in the heel of your left boot. Unfortunately, due to the remoteness of the island and the size of the communicator, it will only be effective when a satellite passes directly overhead and only for about thirty seconds. Plan B involves you hiding Avery in a safe place while Markham hopefully has a meltdown and uses a satellite phone or some other device to connect to the outside world. If he does that, RITA might be able to infiltrate his local area network," he said with a grin.

"Once we know that you and Avery are safe, we'll alert Teriff and Merrick. They will be waiting with a squadron of warriors to evacuate you both," Cosmos continued.

"Cosmos will also have a team ready to prevent issues with Earth's governments," Terra added.

"We'll see you soon," Cosmos said with a reassuring smile.

19

Avery bit back a groan as she slowly fought her way to consciousness. She rolled onto her side and winced. Her head felt like someone had stuffed cotton into it.

Her hand went to her shoulder. Under her shirt, she felt a bandage. Sweat beaded on her brow despite the chill in the room. She forced herself to sit up. A slow look around showed that she was back in her prison cell.

Her fingers trembled as she lifted them to her aching brow. She took a moment to evaluate her body. Lowering her hand, she carefully unbuttoned her blouse far enough to push the material to the side.

The white strip of gauze and medical tape was new. She slowly pulled the tape back to reveal five neat stitches. A frown creased her brow as she tried to remember how she had been injured.

The sound of footsteps approaching alerted her that she was about to have company. She pulled her shirt back over her shoulder and buttoned it. Drawing in a deep breath to stave off the feeling of weakness still weighing her down, she swung her legs over the side of the bed and unsteadily rose to her feet.

"Ah, you are awake," Markham replied with a pleased nod.

"What... what in the hell did you do to me?" she demanded in a voice that was surprisingly hoarse.

"I merely wanted to tip the scales in my favor for the hunt that is about to begin," Markham replied.

She swayed and lifted her hand to her shoulder. "What did you do to me, you sorry-ass piece of shit?"

Markham shook his head. "Such language. Be careful, Ms. Lennox. I detest vulgarities from a woman," he commented.

Avery bit back the caustic response that was on the tip of her tongue. She walked toward the barred door. Several feet away from it, she stopped and looked at him through narrowed eyes.

"What hunt?" she asked through gritted teeth.

The amusement on Markham's face disappeared. His eyes glittered with malice and a sick, anticipatory pleasure. Avery could feel the change in him as well as see it.

"The Game; cat and mouse; survival of the fittest—or should I say the smartest—call it whatever you like. I prefer to think of it as The Hunt. The dance between predator and prey is one of the oldest dances in the world. Nothing makes it more thrilling than when two predators face off against each other," he replied.

The fury that had been building over the last ten days erupted. She surged forward and reached through the bars, ignoring the pain in her shoulder when the sutured area hit the cold metal. Her only thought was finding a way to snap Markham's neck.

He released a taunting chuckle and stepped back out of her reach. His eyes glittered with cruelty.

Her lips twisted into a mocking smile. "He'll kill you in ways you never knew a person could die. He's faster, smarter, and deadlier than any predator on this entire planet," Avery ruthlessly vowed.

"I imagine everything you are saying is true, but we both know he has a weakness, don't we?" he replied with a smirk.

Avery swallowed when he lifted a small black remote and stepped closer to her. She gripped the bar with her right hand. Her left shoulder throbbed. Her eyes remained glued to the device in his hand.

"What have you done?" she whispered.

He stopped a foot from the bars. "I would show you, but I'm afraid the demonstration would put an end to my plans for you. You are the bait, my dear. If your alien doesn't follow the rules, one press of a button and the small capsule inside your body will detonate. You'll feel pain at first, very similar to being shot. Do you remember what that feels like, Ms. Lennox? When a bullet pierces your flesh, cutting through tissue, muscle, and bone before exiting your body?" he inquired.

"How… how do you know about that?" she demanded, tearing her eyes from the device to his face.

"I have friends in the right places, Ms. Lennox. I know about your poor mother and father. I know about how they fell in love while on a mission and wanted to disappear. They wanted a normal life—and then they had you. That was their biggest mistake. Your parents had a chance of disappearing until they had you. You were *their* weakness too, Avery. You are what brought them out into the open," he said in a soft, cruel tone.

Avery released her grip on the bar, and smirked ruefully, returning his stare with a cool one of her own. She didn't miss the confusion that flashed through his eyes.

"Is this the part where I'm supposed to break down in tearful self-doubt and guilt? I'd be happy to, but I'm not a very good actress. My parents made their choices and they lived—and died—because of them. They never once regretted having me. Shit happens in life. We all make our own rules. They made theirs and I've made mine. If anyone has Mommy issues, I think you should take a look in the mirror—or better yet, go have a talk with the bitch in the glass cabinet. I'm sure she'll be as interested in you now as she was when you were growing up," she retorted.

For a moment, Avery wondered if she'd gone too far. The expression on his face twisted into pure hatred, and his fingers twitched on the detonator as he swiftly lifted it in agitation. She instinctively stiffened—waiting for the burst of pain.

"I look forward to killing you, Ms. Lennox. Think about how you'd like your body to be displayed—which will it be? Held in a passionate embrace in your alien lover's arms or sobbing over his dead body?" he asked.

Avery kept her lips pursed together. Markham turned when they heard footsteps approaching. The man she had seen downstairs earlier, the one who had conveniently lifted the lid on the weapons crate in time to let her see what was inside, was walking toward them.

"The helicopter is about to land," the man stated.

Markham nodded. "Take her to the starting point and tell your men to get into position. No one is allowed to kill the alien but me," he ordered.

"Yes, sir." The man glanced at her. "What about the woman?"

Markham turned and looked at Avery for a moment with a calculating stare. She ignored him, her gaze moving over the mercenary. The tattoo on his arm indicated he was ex-American military.

"Once the hunt begins, she is fair game to anyone who wants to kill her," Markham replied.

The man smiled and nodded. "I'll let the men know. I'll inform you the moment she is secured," he added.

"What's your name?" Avery suddenly asked.

The man looked at her with a frown. "Why?" he demanded.

Avery lifted her right hand and gently rubbed her fingers along the bar. She tilted her head, a mocking smirk curving her lips when his expression became uneasy.

"I'd like to know your name so that I can whisper it in your ear when I slit your throat," she replied.

"Grant, take care of her," Markham snapped before turning on his heel. He waved the black box as he walked away. A sense of power swept through Avery. The two men were rattled.

"Put your wrists together. If you move, I'll beat the shit out of you," Grant ordered.

Avery smiled and placed her wrists together so he could restrain them. "Now, Grant, is that any way to treat a lady?" she replied.

Core stared out of the window of the humans' flying machine. Three of Markham's men—Owens, Carter, and Bradley— were sitting across from him, their gazes unwaveringly focused on him. He could not care less about them. His sole focus was on finding Avery and making sure that she was alright.

The moment they swept over the island's cliff, he felt their connection. His fingers curled into his palm as a surge of relief flooded his mind and body. He immediately reached out to her.

Are you injured? Core demanded.

Avery's dry, relieved chuckle echoed through his mind. *I've been better. Markham is insane. He plans to hunt us both down and kill us like some kind of trophy hunting game,* she replied.

You did not answer me. Did he harm you? he gently pressed.

No, except for my pride. I should have known Albertson was up to something. That slimy little weasel set me up, she replied.

I will be with you soon. They are landing the machine, he said.

Core..., she murmured.

Yes, ku lei, he said.

Ta me ja'te.

Her quietly thought words, spoken in his language, tore at his heart. *Ta me ja'te, je talli,* he replied. I love you, my heart.

His softly conveyed words were wrapped with warmth and distracted her while he took into himself the pain she was trying to hide from him.

The slight bump of the skids on the concrete landing site alerted him that they had arrived. The door to the aircraft opened. Owens motioned for him to disembark.

Core released the harness securing him and rose to his feet. Ducking his head, he jumped to the tarmac and strode toward the vehicle waiting for him. The men from the helicopter followed behind him. He straightened and turned when he was clear of the rotating blades. The helicopter rose and soon disappeared back the way it had come.

"Move," Owens ordered.

Core looked down at the man, and gave the mercenary a sharp-toothed grin as his canines lengthened. Owens swallowed while the other two men took a step back, lifted their weapons, and aimed them at his chest.

"I will enjoy killing each and every one of you," he promised them.

"Move or I'll shoot you now," Owens growled.

Core walked over to the back of the truck and climbed into the back. The three men, along with four additional mercenaries who had been standing near the truck, climbed in behind him. Sitting back, he grinned at Owens.

"I can smell your fear, human. I wonder if you will piss your pants when you know you are about to die," he taunted.

"Shut up," Owens muttered. The man pointed his gun at Core's knee.

"Let him try to kill you, Owens. What you don't know, asshole, is that Markham put an acid bomb in your girlfriend. All Markham's got to do is press a button and your gal's insides will melt like butter on a hot stove. Hope you like your women well tenderized," Carter chuckled.

Fury burst through Core. He immediately reached out to Avery. He felt her gentle touch and sigh of resignation.

Did Markham put an explosive inside your body? he demanded.

Yes. My hands aren't free right now so I can't see if I can remove it, she admitted.

Do not try until I find you. How is it activated? he asked.

Markham has a small black detonator. I don't know how many detonators he might have. I know he has at least one on him, she answered.

He could feel her exhaustion. *Where are you now?* he asked.

They have me chained to a set of poles in the middle of the island. Unfortunately, they forgot to leave the keys, she added with dry humor.

I will find you, he swore.

I know you will. I'm going to try to rest. I have a feeling I'm going to need it, she reluctantly admitted.

Core sent another wave of warmth to her before he pulled away. A sense of loss swept through him again as she quietly slipped away from him. The explosive device Markham had placed inside Avery complicated things. He would need to assess a way to remove it from her before Markham had a chance to activate it. For the moment, the human held the advantage.

But not for long, he vowed as his gaze moved to the fortress on the cliff.

20

The truck passed under the opening in the stone wall that fortified three sides of the fortress. Core swiftly analyzed the defenses. The men relied heavily on the wall to protect the interior structures. There were two turrets, each containing a man and a large mounted weapon.

Core inspected the front of the fortress when the truck pulled to a stop. Another mercenary soldier stood near the entrance. So far, he'd counted almost a dozen men.

The ones called Carter and Bradley jumped out of the truck. Owens motioned for him to follow the two men. He rose and jumped to the ground. Out of the corner of his eye, he watched Owens and the rest of the men. Then he recognized Markham standing in the doorway. RITA had displayed his image when they were searching for Merrick.

Core started to take a step forward when Owens stepped in his way. He looked down at the man. Owens sneered.

"You don't move unless I say you can move," Owens gloated.

Core's hand shot out and gripped the man's throat. He lifted Owens off his feet until the smaller man's head was almost level with his. Owens' feet dangled in the air and he frantically clawed at Core's hand as it slowly crushed his windpipe.

"Tell me to move now," Core baited.

"Stand down," Markham loudly ordered when the other soldiers surrounded him.

Core looked back at Markham when he lifted up a small black device for Core to see.

"I would cooperate—unless your feelings for Ms. Lennox aren't as strong as I thought. If that is the case, she would be of no more use to me," Markham said.

With a low snarl, Core tossed Owens body away from him. Owens rolled several times before he lay still in the dirt. Core returned his attention to Markham.

"I am here. State what you want," Core ordered.

"I make the rules here. What is your name, alien?" Markham demanded.

Core sighed. The human would have the upper hand as long as he held the device that could kill Avery, but Markham would never truly be in charge—not as long as Core was alive.

"I am Core Ta'Duran," he replied.

Markham nodded in satisfaction and turned his attention to Carter. The group of soldiers was still standing ready to shoot him.

"Restrain him, scan him for weapons again, then escort him to my study," Markham ordered.

"Yes, sir. What about Owens?" Carter asked, nodding to his fallen comrade.

Markham waved a dismissive hand in the direction of the unconscious man. "If he wakes, send him out first. I have no use for weak men," he replied before turning and disappearing back inside the fortress.

Carter turned to him, and gestured with the tip of his gun. Core started to raise his arms in front of him when Carter shook his head.

"Behind you. I'm not going to risk you breaking my neck. Cuff him," Carter growled.

Core placed his hands behind his back. He grinned when the man trying to restrain him cursed. The silver cuffs they had were not large enough to go around his wrists. A moment later, he felt a tug and the bite of plastic into his skin. They had used a tie similar to the ones Borj told him Hannah had used on him. Unlike Borj, though, they didn't hit him upside the head with a frying pan and knock him out. That would be their first of many mistakes.

Carter motioned for a man to come forward. The man swept a long, flat detection wand over Core's body, then he stepped back. A second man gingerly patted him down, then moved back, and nodded to Carter. Carter motioned toward the steps leading into the fortress.

He strode up the steps and into the fortress. Unlike the medieval exterior, the inside was ultra-modern. Polished marble floors gleamed under hand woven carpet runners. Paintings, sculptures, and elegant porcelain vases—many of which he suspected were valuable to humans—were displayed throughout the interior. He focused on the large center staircase when Carter began climbing the steps and followed when Bradley prodded the tip of his weapon into his back.

At the top of the staircase, the group turned to the left. They proceeded down the large corridor to the double doors at the end of the passage. Core mentally catalogued the details of the room's interior when they entered. The stuffed wildlife carcasses were an atrocity. This man clearly had no respect for anyone but himself.

Markham stood near the fireplace, and when the human didn't speak, Core looked more closely at the frozen form of the woman in the display case, then averted his eyes from the grotesque display. Markham had turned and was watching him with an assessing expression.

"I would offer you a drink, but something tells me now is not the time to release you," Markham said with an almost amused smile.

"I can kill you without spilling the liquor," Core taunted.

Markham chuckled. "I'm sure you could," he replied.

Core's gaze moved to Markham's hand. He was turning the small black box over and over in his hand. When Markham noticed where Core was looking, he lifted the box.

"An insurance policy," Markham commented before he slid the box into the pocket of his jacket.

"What do you want?" Core demanded.

Markham walked away from the fireplace and over to the large desk. His fingers trailed along the polished surface of the dark wood before he waved a hand at the painting. Core's eyes followed the movement.

"I come from a family of hunters, Mr. Ta'Duran. Unlike my predecessors, the hunt is more than the thrill of the kill for me. I enjoy matching wits with my opponents. I've hunted and killed some of the most dangerous animals in the world, but, alas, I've grown bored." Markham turned to face him. Core grimaced with disgust when Markham took his time looking at Core from head to toe. "When I found the other of your kind, I realized that there was finally a predator out there that might actually give me a challenge," he said.

"You want to hunt me—like one of your animals?" Core questioned with a dawning sense of understanding.

"Yes. Two predators pitting their strengths, their skills, and their intelligence against each other," Markham agreed.

"Why didn't you hunt Merrick when you had the chance?" he asked.

Distaste crossed Markham's face. "Unfortunately, I never mix business with pleasure. Once my client found out about your comrade, he offered a price that was too generous to refuse. There was a clause in my contract that I could... regain possession of Merrick when my client was finished with him. Sadly, it looked like the alien wouldn't survive the good doctor's treatment, but then," he said with a smile, "CRI raided the complex and rescued the man—and the little housekeeper he was enamored with," he added, waving his hand dismissively.

Core growled and Markham's smile widened. "Imagine my delight when there was more than one alien at Banks' cottage. Merrick may be gone now, but you're here now, aren't you? One of your kind steps out of the ring, and another steps in. Tell me, what *is* your species called?" Markham asked.

Core's patience was beginning to wear thin. Avery was chained somewhere on the island with an explosive device inside her and Markham was acting as if they were having social hour. If Markham wanted to hunt, then it was time to start the game.

Clenching his fists, Core took a deep breath through his nose and flexed the muscles in his arms. The thick plastic bands cut into his skin, then they snapped. He casually pulled his wrists up and rubbed one of them.

"I come from a world of warriors. Our species is Prime. My world is called Baade. I am a leader of my clan. I do not care if you know this because by the time I am finished, every single one of you will be dead. If you think you are such a fierce hunter, then shut up and let the hunt begin," Core snarled, allowing his teeth to elongate. The men behind Markham moved warily back several steps, but Markham just pulled the small black box out of his pocket and held it so that Core could see it, chuckling to himself as he did so.

"As a matter of sportsmanship and to make the hunt more interesting, I'm giving you a twenty minute head start before my men leave to kill Ms. Lennox. If she is still chained to the poles where we left her, she'll die there. In forty-eight hours if she is still alive, I'm going to depress the button on this remote. The capsule implanted in her will explode and release an acid that will seep into her bloodstream, causing her to die an excruciatingly painful death," Markham explained in a hard tone.

"What guarantee do I have that you won't kill her sooner?" Core demanded.

Markham smiled. "None," he replied before nodding to Carter. "Make sure he is escorted to the gate. The countdown starts the moment you pass through it."

Core turned on his heel. He had to find Avery, get her to safety, and remove the capsule. Striding down the corridor, he ignored the men jogging to keep up with him. His focus was on his mate.

Once out in the courtyard, he paused and looked up. Markham was watching him from the upper window. Core glanced at the men warily watching him before he looked at the turrets. A sense of determination swept through him.

Avery, ku lei, I am coming he promised as he crossed under the arch. *I need you to guide me to you,*

A weak chuckle slipped into his mind. *I'll be chilling out and dreaming about how we're going to kill all of these bastards until you get here,* she tiredly responded.

21

"Bloody hell, but I'm going to kill that bastard slowly," Avery muttered under her breath.

The shivers that had started earlier were constant now. She felt like someone had placed her feet on an electric mat and was having fun at her expense by turning the power on and off. No sooner would one mass of shakes end than the next one started.

Her blood had congealed around the ripped sutures in her shoulder. The gauze taped to her skin was no match for her oozing blood or the cold weather. The psycho bastards had an awful sense of humor. They had placed the key to locks holding her within view, but far enough away there was no way she would ever be able to reach them, even if she were able to free one arm.

Concern gripped her that she was beginning to succumb to hypothermia. Her mind was growing foggy and her fingers and toes had become numb an hour ago. She tried to shift to ease the burden on her aching arms, but instead her knees trembled and threatened to give out on her. Locking them, she clenched her jaw. Her head was starting to sag when she suddenly felt a surge of warmth and energy flood her.

Avery, ku lei, I am coming. I need you to guide me to you, Core's tender voice filtered through her mind.

She lifted her head and looked over the open area. Hope and a renewed determination filled her. There was about to be a war and she wasn't going to miss it if she could help it. A small, dry chuckle slipped from her lips at the thought.

I'll be chilling out and dreaming about how we're going to kill all of these bastards until you get here, she responded.

She closed her eyes and focused on pulling on the mental silver thread that connected them. She'd lead him to her position and once she was free, they were going to do some serious ass-kicking. Focusing on the details of the route the men had taken earlier to her location, she kept the image in her mind so that Core could access it.

Breaking into a fast run, Core's long legs covered the uneven ground. He heard the startled shout from one of the men in the turret when the man saw how fast he could run.

Ordinarily he would have preferred to keep such a skill hidden from the humans since the surprise factor might have come in handy later. Such luxuries were not an option at the moment. Besides, he reasoned, Markham had been involved with the experimentation on Merrick. He probably already knew how fast a Prime could run.

His connection with Avery pulled him to the north. He could see the rough road in her mind. Concerned that the road would not be a straight path to her, he focused on what she was mentally envisioning and compared it to the holographic map that RITA had shown him.

He estimated that he would have approximately seven and a half hours before the next satellite passed overhead and he could contact the others. Once he had Avery and could access the beacon in his heel, he'd know for sure. The beacon had a visible count down until the next satellite sync. Regardless of how much time they had left, it would be a moot point unless he could remove or deactivate the capsule inside Avery. There was no way he could risk alerting the others while Markham could still activate the device.

A thick blanket of menacing clouds had rolled across the sky since he arrived on the island. The wind had also picked up and the temperature was beginning to significantly drop. A new concern struck him as he ran. Avery was exposed to the elements.

Avery, love, I am almost there, he promised.

Fear rose inside him when she didn't answer. He could still feel their connection, but it was very weak. He pushed his body faster than he'd ever gone before. Behind him, he could hear the whine of vehicles. They were using motorcycles instead of the large, slower transports.

Running uphill, he maneuvered through a series of boulders. Once he crested the top, he could see a narrow valley. In the center of the valley was a platform—beneath which Avery hung limply between two poles.

Avery, I see you, he urgently said.

What... took you... so long? she tried to tease, but the words were slurred and broken.

Relief swept through him when he saw her head lift for a moment before she lowered it again. He covered the ground between them swiftly, thanks in large part to the fact that he was moving downhill. He estimated he had only minutes to free her and disappear into the rocky terrain surrounding them.

"Avery, my love," Core said, reaching the platform.

He jumped up onto the wooden structure and cupped her frozen face between his warm hands. A soft moan escaped her. She turned her lips into his palm.

"Key... Key on post," she forced through stiff lips.

He turned to look for what she was talking about. In front of her was a low post with a hook. On it was a key. He quickly released her to retrieve the key.

Seconds later, she was lying limply in his arms. Her face was white and there were pinched lines of pain around her mouth. She was breathing with quick, shallow breaths.

"Avery, I have to get you out of here. The other men will be here shortly," he urgently murmured, hoping his body heat would raise her temperature quickly.

She forced her eyes open. "Markham... is hunting us," she whispered.

"He only thinks he is," he teased.

A hint of a smile tugged at her lips. "Can you carry me until I get my body to work?" she asked.

"To the ends of the universe and back if necessary," he promised.

"God, I've been such an idiot," she muttered.

He rose to his feet with Avery cradled in his arms. Regret poured through him when he jumped down from the platform. He hated jarring her, but at the moment, speed was essential to their survival.

I wish I could block all of your pain, he said with regret.

Don't. It helps remind me that I'm alive. How far behind you were Markham's men? she asked.

Not far, he replied.

She trembled in his arms. He needed to find a place to hide them so he could tend her injuries. His gaze swept over the rugged surroundings. They were in a narrow cut between the rocks that he was sure would abruptly end. Their only option was to go up.

His assumption was proven correct when he saw the dead end ahead. He slowed and gently lowered her to the ground. She leaned back against a boulder and held her left arm close to her body.

"Please tell me that you have weapons or a miracle or two in your back pocket," she sighed.

He grinned down at her and pulled one of the buckles on the side of his vest free as well as a strip of leather that he wound around his wrist. Pinching the end, he pulled some of the fine wire free. He created a knot and slid it over the notch of a small, black grappling hook that looked like a decoration on the strip of leather he had wound around his wrist.

He pressed the release, and the slender grappling hook shot upward. When it disappeared over a large rock outcropping, he jerked on the wire.

Satisfaction coursed through him when he felt it snag and hold. Bending, he hooked the wire to the side of his boot, and created another loop so he could slip his foot into the stirrup that he'd created. Next, he pulled a fingerless glove from his vest and slipped it on.

Turning, he reached down to Avery. In the distance, they could hear the roar of the motorcycles drawing closer. She looked up at him with a confused expression.

"I don't think that piece of sewing thread can handle our combined weight," she protested.

He wiggled his fingers and winked at her. "Maybe not if it was from your world—or from someone other than Cosmos," he teased.

Her lips curved into a rueful smile. She placed her icy fingers in his, moaning softly at the pleasure of the warmth in his hand. He pulled her up and wrapped his arm around her waist.

"I'm not sure I have the strength at the moment to hold onto you," she admitted, shakily standing on his boot.

"I'll do the holding," he promised.

Looking up, he pulled the thread taut. Immediately, they rose up off the ground. He could feel the friction warmth of the wire as it slid against his protected palm.

When they reached the top, he braced his legs against the side of the rock face, and steadied Avery as she clumsily crawled upward, using his body as a ladder. Only when she had disappeared over the edge did he pull himself up and over after her. He quickly retrieved the grappling hook and replaced the buckle on his vest.

Avery sat huddled next to the boulders. He could see her slender shoulders shaking and hear the chattering of her teeth. He unbuttoned his vest and pulled off the long-sleeved shirt under it. Kneeling, he gently helped her slip on his warm shirt over her clothing.

"What... what about... you?" she asked.

He smoothed his hand over her cheek. "Our body temperatures run warmer than yours. I'll keep the vest as it has most of our weapons integrated into it. You can have the shirt," he said.

They both turned their heads when they heard the motorcycles in the valley below as they reached the dead end. Core stood and peered over the side. Three men sat on the machines looking around them.

"They had to have come this way," one of the men shouted above the noise.

A second spun his motorcycle in a tight circle until he was facing the way they had come. Core pulled back, his gaze on the cliff wall across from them. There was a fissure. If he could set off an explosive in it, there was a good possibility that the entire shelf would collapse. He reached down and pulled one of the buttons off of the front of his vest. Twisting it first one way and then the other, he threw the small explosive with the precision of a major league baseball pitcher.

The tiny black button disappeared into the black hole before slowly rolling back down. It caught on the bottom edge against a small rock. Core bent and grabbed his vest. Sliding it on, he turned and scooped Avery back up into his arm. Ahead of him was a sheltering cluster of trees.

He had only taken a few steps when the explosive detonated. He listened to the hoarse shouts of alarm before they were drowned out by the avalanche of rock. A flash of lightning lit the dark sky. They made it to the cluster of trees just as the first cold raindrops began to fall.

22

"What I wouldn't give for one of Cosmos' Gateway devices right about now," Avery murmured with a sigh.

She stared out at the rain. How Core had created a shelter out of the limited natural materials available was beyond her. She was good at a lot of things, but creating an adequate shelter out of tree branches and leaves would be pushing it. If he started a fire with two sticks, she would be completely in awe of him—not that she wasn't already.

"I like that you are in awe of me," he chuckled, settling on the ground next to her.

"You aren't supposed to hear things like that," she grumbled.

He reached over and brushed her hair back from where it was stuck to her damp cheek. He frowned when he felt the heat radiating from her skin even though she was still shivering uncontrollably. Lifting her chin, he gazed into her glazed eyes with a worried expression.

"You are running a fever," he said.

She nodded. "I know."

"Lay back and let me look at where Markham inserted the capsule," he instructed.

Avery nodded. Pain radiated through her shoulder as he helped her lay down on the chilled ground. She tried not to groan when she felt the dampness seeping through her wool pants.

Her fingers curled into tight fists as he gently released the fastenings on the shirt he'd given her, then unfastened the buttons on her silk blouse. He pushed the soft material to the side, and caught sight of the bloodied gauze. His eyes blazed with fury. She caressed his cheek.

"At least the tape won't hurt when you pull it off," she tried to joke. Her body convulsed into a mass of shivers, which she was sure didn't help lighten the mood. The only good thing at the moment was that his fingers were warm. She just wished she could bury herself in him to chase away the ice that had settled deep in her bones.

"I need to open the wound to see if I can remove the capsule," he said with an apologetic expression.

"Do it. I'd rather you tried to get it out than leave it to burst inside me," she replied through gritted teeth.

He gave a sharp nod, reached down, and pulled a small razor-sharp blade the size of her little finger out of his boot. She looked up at his face as he leaned over her. A weak smile curved her lips when she felt him in her mind.

I will try to block as much of your pain as I can, he tenderly promised.

"I know you will," she whispered.

Avery closed her eyes and focused on the silver thread that connected them. She fought to keep her body still as he sliced through sutures that were still intact. Warm blood flowed sluggishly over her chilled skin.

A tear escaped and she bit down on her lip to keep from making any noise. The sound of rolling thunder and the torrential downpour would probably conceal any noise that she made, but she didn't want to take any unnecessary chances. Markham was not the type of man to delay because of a rain storm.

Black spots danced behind her eyelids when she felt Core probing her wound. The blackness exploded into a fiery display of red when his finger finally touched the capsule. Her lips parted in a gasp before Avery sank into the inky black abyss of unconsciousness.

Core shifted Avery on his lap and slowly withdrew his teeth from her jugular. He held her close against his warm body and made sure that his shirt still covered as much of her as it could. Relief washed through him when he noticed that her skin did not seem to be radiating quite as much heat as it had been. The nanobots were doing their job.

Lifting his shirt, he gently pulled back her silk blouse and peeked at the wound on her shoulder. The skin was already beginning to heal. Readjusting her clothing, he leaned back against the tree and laid his cheek against her hair, his strong arms holding her close.

The thumb-sized cylinder had been difficult to pull out. His gaze moved to the blood-covered piece of metal shaped like a lozenge. He hated to think of what Avery would have endured if Markham had followed through on his threat to release the acid.

He lifted his hand and looked at the readout on the small beacon. They had six hours before it could be triggered—six hours to evade Markham and his men. They had two choices. They could run, hide, and hope they could stay alive long enough to contact Cosmos and have a portal opened. Or, they could turn the tables by hunting and taking out Markham and his men.

I like the second option better, Avery silently voiced her preference.

A deep laugh shook his body and he rubbed his cheek against her hair. *Has anyone ever told you that you are a bloodthirsty woman?* he inquired.

No. They all wanted to live, she replied.

How are you feeling? he asked, tilting his head so that he could see her face.

She smiled up at him. “Bloodthirsty—but I wouldn’t say no to a hot shower,” she murmured, sitting up.

She reached for her shoulder, and felt where the capsule had been. She locked eyes with Core, her surprise evident in her expression.

“I removed it,” he replied to her unspoken question.

Her fingers probed the affected area. "It feels like it is completely healed! How can that possibly happen?" she asked.

He smiled and brushed a kiss across her parted lips. "Nanobots. Terra injected me with them. I transferred them to you. They are designed to repair any injuries and destroy infections. They are only effective for a short time. I will have to let Terra and Cosmos know that they worked as they predicted," he mused.

"I'll have to add my personal approval," she said before laying her head against his chest. "I finally understand why after all these years."

He frowned and grasped her fingers when she lifted them to rub against his chest. He pressed a kiss to her fingertips.

"What do you finally understand?" he asked.

"Why my parents did the things they did. Why they were willing to give up everything—to have everything. Why they were willing to risk their lives to have a life," she quietly answered.

"Why?" he murmured.

"Because they understood how empty life was otherwise. They knew that love, marriage, having a family—me—was worth any risk. I couldn't understand why they would believe that—until I felt it myself," she confessed.

He nudged her fingers open with his nose and pressed a kiss to the center of her palm over the mark that declared they were a match. A sense of peace flowed through him and he knew that it was not his emotions that he was feeling, but Avery's.

"I can't have children," she said with regret.

"If we want children, we can borrow one. The good thing is we can give them back and I can have you all to myself," he assured her.

Avery chuckled. "How long before we can get off of this miserable piece of rock?" she asked.

"Six hours," he ruefully replied.

He hugged her close when she softly cursed. His mate didn't whine; she cursed and fought like a warrior. She didn't run from her problems; she met them head on.

"What kind of weapons do you have?" she finally asked, sitting up and looking at him.

"Enough to make Markham wish he'd chosen someone else to hunt," he commented.

"You have a plan, don't you?" she said more than asked.

He nodded. "Yes. It is time for Markham to encounter a true predator," he said with a flash of his sharp teeth.

23

Avery scanned the area, trying to find Core. She kept her hand pressed against the patch like he'd told her to. She hadn't understood why he'd given it to her until he'd demonstrated how it worked. Cosmos always made the coolest toys.

Now, she knelt on the ground, invisible to the two men as they slowly ambled closer to her location as they searched for her. They each wore a black knit cap that completely covered their heads, leaving only their eyes clear of the fabric. Their eyes were shielded by clear goggles. She really hoped that they weren't thermal.

A slight movement caught her attention. She would have missed Core crouching on the limb above the men if she hadn't known he was somewhere close by. The moment the second man passed under him, Core silently dropped down. His large hands grasped the man's head and he snapped the mercenary's neck with a firm twist.

The man's partner turned with his weapon at the ready. Avery stood up and pulled her hand away from the patch so she would suddenly appear in the man's peripheral vision. Core reached out and grabbed the end of the soldier's rifle as he reflexively turned toward Avery. Caught off guard between the two of them, he hesitated. That hesitation gave Core the opportunity to shove the end of the weapon into the enemy's nose.

Avery heard the crunch of the man's nose as it shattered. The blow caused the soldier to release his grip on his rifle. Core rotated the weapon and fired a single shot into the man's chest as he fell to the ground.

Core's accusing gaze swung to her. "You were supposed to stay concealed," he growled, stepping over the dead man as he walked toward her.

She grinned and shrugged. "It's called teamwork. He sensed you were there. I like you much better without any bullet holes in you," she stated with a pat to his chest.

She saw his lips part and knew he was about to retort with a caustic remark, but her attention was suddenly diverted by a slight whistling sound. She lurched forward and wrapped her arms around Core's waist, pushing him down to the ground seconds before a ball of fire exploded against the tree where she had been kneeling.

Core rolled and covered her body with his when another firebomb exploded to the left of them. He lifted his head as she exclaimed, "They must have been wearing bodycams. We've got to get out of here."

They got to their feet as smoke and flames roiled in the air. Core reached for her hand, and started to pull her forward when she realized she had dropped the patch.

"Leave it," Core ordered.

She shook her head. "We may need it. Besides, we can't leave this kind of technology behind," she said, twisting around. She grabbed the patch and shoved it in her pocket before picking up the rifle Core had taken from the man. Placing her hand in his again, she motioned with her chin she was ready. "Now we can go."

Core released a low curse, and Avery bit back her grin. She needed to focus on their escape. They swerved to the right as another burst of flames exploded. The bastards were using napalm laced rounds to insure that the wet timber would burn.

The ground soon began to slope upward. She pulled her hand free of Core's and slung the rifle's carrying strap over her shoulder so she could use both hands to help her climb. A steep, narrow track, probably used by wildlife on the island, wound through the thick plants growing among the rocks.

Soon they were above the forest. From here the whole area looked like an inferno. Avery fought the urge to cough as they found cover behind several large boulders. Peering around the rocks, she saw four vehicles lined up on the other side of the woods.

This group of men was larger. Two of the vehicles had cannons mounted to the back. That was what they were using to demolish the forest. She could see several of the men spread out in a formation ready to advance once the fire died down.

She looked at Core when he removed his vest and quickly began pulling off items. It took a second for her to realize what he was assembling. Her eyebrows rose in surprise when less than a minute later, he had a bow and a handful of short but lethal arrows

"Pull four of the buttons from my vest," he instructed.

"What are you going to do?" she asked.

He nodded in the direction of the vehicles. "If you twist the top of the button to the left, then back to the right, it will activate the explosive inside. I think it only right that if we have to walk, so should they," he said with a wink.

She laughed softly, and peered over the boulder with a raised eyebrow. Looking back at him, she gave him a skeptical look.

"Do you think you can shoot those that far?" she queried in a doubtful tone, looking at the small arrows.

This time he chuckled. "Laser guided," he retorted with a wink.

She whistled under her breath. "Cosmos really has been holding back some of the shit he has been learning from your world," she muttered under her breath.

"On my mark," Core said with a nod. "Now."

Avery quickly turned the top of the button left, then right, and held up the powerful explosive she'd activated. Core touched the tip of the arrow to the bomb. A strong magnet pulled the device out of her hand and to the arrow's head. Core aimed the weapon at the first vehicle and released the arrow.

They repeated the process three more times. By the time the last arrow was released, the first vehicle had already exploded. Avery watched in awe as each vehicle lifted up into the air before falling backwards. The men inside and those manning the cannons hadn't stood a chance. Seconds after the initial explosion, the rest of their munitions inside ignited.

Those fortunate to be far enough away to survive the explosions never heard the whiz of the bullets that cut them down. Avery carefully aimed at the remaining line of men and fired with the skill of a sniper. She paused, adjusted the scope, and peered down to scan the flat plateau. At the far end she could see another vehicle. Her eyes narrowed when she saw Markham standing on the sidelines, watching their systematic elimination of his men.

Avery focused the crosshairs on the man's chest. Her finger slowly squeezed on the trigger as she held her breath. It would be an impossible shot from this distance, but she had to attempt it. Her finger depressed the trigger, but nothing happened—the chamber was empty.

Avery lowered the rifle, her gaze still locked on Markham until she felt Core's hand on her arm. Turning to look at him, she saw the same grim determination on his face.

"Now we hunt," he quietly said.

Five hours later, the four-wheel drive vehicle slid through the narrow entrance of the fortress and came to a stop. Karl ordered the soldier sitting in the back seat to get out of the vehicle. Bradley opened the door and half stepped half fell out onto the ground. Karl dispassionately watched as Bradley stumbled toward the open arch of the entrance. All of his other men were gone—destroyed by the alien and Avery Lennox.

Bradley manually activated the heavy metal gate, and Owens

pulled up in front of the stronghold Karl called home. He opened the passenger side door and stepped out of the vehicle.

"Bradley, man the turret," Karl ordered.

Bradley opened his mouth to reply, then his eyes widened in shock and he fell forward. There was a long thin black shaft protruding from the center of his back.

"Owens, take the turret. Carter, follow me," Karl snarled, turning to ascend the steps into the fortress.

Carter scanned the area as he cautiously moved up the steps behind him. Karl pushed the massive steel door open and entered. Anger burned deep inside him. He'd been thwarted at each attempt to track down and kill the two of them, his prey.

By the time he made the decision to retreat to a more contained area, half the men who had been with him were already eliminated.

If you can't find the lion, bring him to you, Markham thought.

The alien and Lennox reminded him of the story of the Tsavo Man-Eaters. This time he would be the bait that would draw them in, and like Patterson, he would be waiting for them.

Karl tucked his rifle under his arm and pulled his gloves off as he strode across the foyer. Carter followed closely behind him. He paused on the first step and turned to the other man.

"Seal the fortress," Karl ordered.

"Yes, sir," Carter replied with a curt nod.

Carter double checked the entry doors to make sure they were secure before he disappeared down the corridor to the security room. Karl took the stairs leading up to his office two at a time.

As he strode down the corridor, he thought about everything that had happened since he had released the alien. In less than five hours he was down to three—no, now two men. The alien bastard and Lennox had systematically eliminated each man with surgical precision.

What infuriated him the most was that he should have had the upper hand. This was his sanctuary. He knew the island well, its hazards and the shelters it could provide outside the fortress.

He slipped his hand into his pocket and touched the detonator for the capsule he had implanted in Lennox. As tempting as it was to kill the woman, he refrained from doing it. If he couldn't kill the bastard, holding Avery Lennox's life in the palm of his hand might be the only ace he had up his sleeve.

Karl looked up at the painting of his mother as he entered his office. Her mocking gaze stared down at him, heating his blood with hatred. He didn't bother to close the doors. Either he would escape before the alien and Lennox made it into the fortress or he would kill them once they entered this room.

It seemed only fitting that the hunt should end in this room. This was the last resting place of his kills. He refused to consider the idea that he might not survive this competition.

Walking around his desk, he propped his hunting rifle against the gleaming mahogany. He opened the top drawer and pulled out a remote. Turning, he pointed it at the painting behind him. The painting rotated back into the wall and a series of screens appeared. Each screen depicted a different section of the fortress—both inside and out.

His gaze focused on the empty turrets. A second screen showed Owens lying lifeless on the ground a few feet from Bradley. A movement near the gate showed Lennox squatting near Bradley's body before she removed the dead man's sidearm.

He had underestimated the prim and proper bitch. Watching her efficient and confident movements, he realized now that what he'd taken for elegance and grace was in reality something much deadlier. She was a trained military operative. He recognized the way she had handled herself over the last few hours. Irritation flared inside of him at his miscalculation.

His fingers tapped on his desk as he watched the security cameras. He leaned forward when he saw Carter in the security room, watching the set of monitors there. Karl's mouth tightened when he saw Carter pick up the satellite phone which would be useless for almost another hour until one of the communication satellites came into range.

"You'll be dead before anyone arrives," he commented with a sardonic twist to his lips.

One by one, the cameras on the perimeter went offline. Karl dispassionately watched as Avery Lennox walked up to one of the cameras, stared into it with a smug expression before she lifted the pistol she had taken from Bradley and fired a shot into the center.

"I'm going to enjoy killing that bitch," Karl reflected.

He rose to his feet. The hunting rifle next to his desk would be of little use in the close confines of the fortress. His gaze lit on several weapons in a display cabinet that would work much more effectively.

Sliding his fingers under the lip of his desk, he pressed the small button hidden there. Thick plates of metal slid down over the windows. Only the dim glow from the security monitor provided any light in the room. That was more than enough time to retrieve the items he needed for what he suspected would be the hunt of his life.

~

CRI Headquarters: Houston, Texas:

"I have a connection," Rose called over her shoulder.

"Markham's cell phone?" Cosmos questioned.

Rose shook her head. "No, but the signal is coming from the island. RITA, can you access it?" she asked.

"I'm working on it, sweetheart. Oh, FRED, you are such a naughty program. We're in," RITA announced.

Rose's upper lip curled in disgust. "I don't think I want to know that part of his programming. I wish Amelia hadn't called it a day. She is better at this type of hacking than I am," she muttered.

"I can request that she come back down. She is only a couple of floors from here," Cosmos said.

"She isn't in the building. The signal is fading. We will.... FRED and I were able to upload a small bit of programming, but it will take a while to replicate. I'm not sure how effective it will be. The only potential access was through their security system," RITA replied.

"Was there any information about Core and Avery?" Cosmos quietly asked.

"I'm sorry, Cosmos. There wasn't enough time to search their security system," RITA replied in a mournful tone.

"So, what do we do?" Rose asked, looking up at Cosmos.

He looked at the satellite's position relative to where they needed it to be. "We wait—and hope that Core and Avery are somewhere safe," he said, shoving his hands in his pockets.

"You know, we've got them trapped. We could play it safe and wait for the satellite to pass over, contact Cosmos, and let the cavalry finish this," Avery dryly announced when Core appeared by her side.

He looked at her with a raised eyebrow. "Where is the fun in that?" he teased.

Avery looked at the two dead men lying in the courtyard. She knew for a fact that Markham and one other man were still in the fortress, but she didn't know if there was anyone else inside—perhaps a housekeeper or the chef who'd prepared their meals, or a whole battalion he'd kept in reserve. At this point, she considered everyone hostile.

She looked down at her empty sidearm. She'd taken it off the man that she'd killed with Core's bow and arrow. Cosmos and Terra had outdone themselves this time. She felt like she was in a James Bond movie with all of the amazing gadgets Core had pulled out of his vest and boots over the past several hours. Unfortunately, they were almost out of the fancy gadgets and about to enter the cobra's den.

"They are sure to have the building sealed," she commented, looking at the exterior.

He looked at the massive doors. "I have one explosive left," he said before looking at her. "I will go after Markham. You go after the other soldier."

She looked down in surprise when he held out another sidearm. She took it, and looked up at him with a raised eyebrow.

"Owens didn't need it anymore," he said.

She chuckled. Releasing the magazine, she saw that it had five bullets left. She slid the magazine back into the butt clip and nodded.

"Please be careful. Markham is extremely dangerous. If you get a chance, kill him. You don't want to play with this one," she warned.

"Trust me when I say his death will reflect his life," he vowed.

The expression in his eyes hardened, reminding her of the look on his face before they had gone after Merrick the last time at the cottage. She caressed his cheek. Lifting up onto her toes, she brushed a kiss across his lips.

"Let's end this," she said.

Avery stood back and watched as Core pulled the last explosive button from his vest. He twisted it and tossed it at the front doors. They hid behind a low concrete wall, and the explosion shook the ground. She looked up in time to see one of the front doors tumbling down the steps. Gripping her gun tightly, she followed Core up the stairs and through the entrance into the dim interior toward Markham's last stand.

24

Core instinctively knew where Markham would go. A wounded animal often retreats to its den, and the room where Markham had brought him earlier was the only place Markham truly felt invincible.

He climbed the stairs, pausing briefly to watch as Avery began searching for the remaining soldier. He felt her soothing touch in his mind. She no longer sought to prevent him access. Today had demonstrated that when they were connected, they were a powerful team, a true power couple.

He refocused his attention on Markham. When he reached the top of the stairs, he turned to the open doors at the end of the corridor. The room's interior was dim, the only light coming from a few displays on the wall above the large desk.

His lips twitched in amusement. Prime warriors had very good night vision. Thanks to living deep in the forest, his clan had evolved and were well adapted for moving through the forests at night.

It didn't take long for his eyes to adjust. He paused and listened. He heard a foot scrape against the floor to his left, and picked up the barely audible twang from the release of a string. He twisted to the right just in time to evade the short arrow.

He moved with the agility of a cat when several more arrows were released in rapid succession. Darting forward, he launched himself through the open door and rolled. He stopped near the corner of Markham's desk.

"Rockman was right when she concluded your species had excellent night vision," Markham commented.

Core's eyes narrowed. Markham was using an audio enhancer. His voice echoed throughout the room, making it difficult to pinpoint where he was.

"So this is how a human hunter fights his prey, by hiding in the dark," Core taunted, pushing up until he was in a crouch.

"You would agree that there are some areas where your species has an advantage. I'm merely leveling the playing field," Markham replied.

Core jerked to the side when Markham fired a powerful weapon. The flash of the report briefly blinded him. Bits of wood shattered, sending small slivers into his left arm. He moved farther behind the desk.

"I see that the lovely Ms. Lennox is taking care of my last remaining soldier," Markham commented.

Core frowned and looked up. On the monitors, he could see Avery moving along the dim corridor downstairs. His attention moved to the last monitor which displayed the soldier watching the same feed.

Avery, be careful. There is a man in one of the rooms. He is watching your approach on the security monitor, he warned.

I've got this. You focus on not getting yourself killed, she replied before adding a soft thank you.

Core forced his gaze away from the monitors. A slow smile curved his lips as a new idea came to him. He couldn't tell where Markham was when he spoke, but he could sure as hell hear him when he moved.

Gripping the large office chair, he suddenly rose to his feet and flung it as hard as he could down the room toward the array of display cases. Markham's loud curses followed the sounds of shattering glass.

Core reached down and gripped the desk. He was going to lift it up and use it as a shield when his finger pressed the hidden button under the edge. The grating sound of metal on metal filled the air at the same time as light from the late afternoon sun flooded the room.

The sudden light blinded them both, but Markham made a sound as he instinctively moved backward and Core charged toward it.

Markham flung his night vision goggles off and lifted his hands to brace against Core's forearms. Twisting to the side, Core pulled Markham around, gripped his neck, and pushed him up against the partially destroyed display case holding the remains of Markham's mother and the two lions.

"Stop!" Markham ordered, raising up the detonator he was gripping tightly in his hand.

Core's eyes glittered with malicious triumph.

"Release me or she dies," Markham threatened.

Core took a moment to scrutinize the man's face. Disgust for such cruelty coursed through him.

In the reflection of the glass, he saw a shimmer of light.

"Core!" Merrick called, stepping through the Gateway.

"Release me," Markham hoarsely repeated.

"You have the right to demand justice," Teriff quietly stated. "Both of you do."

A smile curved Core's lips. He held Markham trapped against the glass display case with one hand while he reached into his pocket with his other. He pulled out the small capsule he'd removed from Avery's body, and held it up so Markham could see it.

"How—?" Markham started to ask.

The man's words ended in a choked gag when Core suddenly shoved the capsule into Markham's mouth and released him. He wrapped his hand around Markham's and stared down into the man's eyes as he pressed Markham's thumb down on the detonator.

Markham's mouth opened in a scream that never sounded. The acid was already burning its way down his throat to his vocal cords. Core pushed Markham backwards, and the glass wall of the display case, already weakened, collapsed inward. Markham's writhing body fell over one of the lions. Seconds later, he lay motionless, sightlessly staring up at the face of his dead mother.

"That was nasty," Cosmos said.

Core slowly turned his head to look at the men who had come to help him and Avery. "He was going to use it on Avery," he quietly said before his eyes moved to the monitors. A smile curved his lips when he saw the slumped figure of the soldier in the security room and Avery calmly walking up the stairs with the faint but very familiar figures of RITA and FRED by her side. He turned to look at the three men with a raised eyebrow.

"What took you so long?" he finally demanded.

EPILOGUE

Washington, D.C.

"The Vice-President and now this. It is hard to believe that Public Servants sworn to protect our nation have instead done so much to harm it," President Askew Thomas said with a sigh.

"Do you have any other questions, Mr. President?" Avery asked.

Askew shook his head. A knock sounded on the door leading to the Oval Office, and Askew looked up from the report she had given him. A moment later, his secretary peeked inside.

"Mr. President, Secretary Albertson is here to see you," she announced.

"Askew, how are you doing to… day?" Richmond Albertson's voice faded when he saw Avery serenely sitting on the couch.

"Hello, Richmond," Avery greeted with a slight bow of her head.

"Ms. Lennox… Avery. I thought… I had heard that you…," Richmond stuttered before pursing his lips together.

"Disappeared?" she suggested.

"Askew…," Richmond started to say in a sharp, aggressive tone.

"Don't dig yourself any deeper than you already have, Richmond. I respected you and you let me down," Askew warned, standing up.

Richmond looked at Avery with a flash of hatred, then he glanced behind her and felt pure terror. He backed up against the desk. How had he overlooked the four alien men standing near the wall behind Avery?

"Askew...," Richmond choked.

"I don't think you'd get much satisfaction seeking the Right of Justice with him, Core," Cosmos observed.

Avery felt Core's disgust for the overweight Secretary of State who looked like he was about to have a heart attack. She had to agree with Cosmos. The man was a total waste of space.

I could claim the Right of Justice, but there is no justice in watching a man cower and beg, Core silently conceded.

I told you, she teased.

Avery rose to her feet and stepped forward to shake the President's hand. "I'm sure that Bill can take it from here," she said with a smile directed toward the FBI Director who was sitting in one of the two chairs near the bookcase. Bill Evers nodded. Avery turned and looked at Richmond. Her lip curled with distaste.

"I want you to tell the President and the FBI Director everything—and I mean everything—that you know. If you don't, I'll have my mate drag your sorry ass to a world where no amount of begging or expensive lawyers will save your life," she promised in a soft, menacing tone.

Richmond nodded his head in agreement.

Avery turned and walked around the couch. "Cosmos, I'm taking an extended vacation," she calmly announced.

"I'll let everyone know," Cosmos promised, stepping to the side.

"Tilly is planning another Romantic Comedy weekend. Will you and Terra be there?" Teriff asked.

Cosmos laughed. "Yes, we'll be there," he said.

Avery looked over her shoulder at President Thomas before she bowed her head to the FBI Director. She turned and smiled up at Core when he wrapped his arm around her waist. Teriff opened the Gateway and they all stepped through to the control room on Baade.

A final glance over her shoulder gave her a huge sense of satisfaction —Richmond Albertson lay in a terrified abject heap on the floor of the Oval Office, swearing that he would tell them everything they wanted to know.

Core's Home: Eastern Forest of Baade
Two months later:

"Avery, love, are you awake?"

Avery groaned softly and cracked one eyelid. The blurry image of RITA2 was sitting on the side of her bed. She hadn't been dreaming.

"What do you want? I thought I answered all your questions last night," she moaned, reaching for Core's pillow.

She sighed. It was still warm. She'd felt him get up a few minutes ago.

She pulled the pillow to her and rolled onto her side. Her eyes had just closed again when she heard a giggle from the other room. A frown creased her brow when it was followed by another one.

Avery, I need your help, Core said in a voice tinged with panic.

Her eyes popped open and she scrambled out of the bed. She was only vaguely aware that RITA2 was trying to talk to her. She grabbed her robe and pulled it on as she hurried out of the room.

Where are you? she demanded.

In the living room. Wear your robe, we have company, he warned.

I am, she replied.

She quickly tied the belt of her robe around her waist, and pulled her hair free as she hurried down the landing to the lower level. She was about to demand to know what was wrong again when she saw Angus, Core, and Cosmos standing with their backs to her. She slowed, worry gnawing at her stomach.

"I wasn't sure who I should talk to," RITA2 was saying. "Tilly and Tink are fantastic, but I thought you might be able to talk to Amelia about this. RITA thinks she might be able to figure out what we did. I mean… I'm not sure how this actually happened. DAR and I were only doing some experimental coding. We never expected…." RITA2 was almost babbling.

Avery's lips parted in a gasp when the men moved aside and she could see what they were looking at. Seated on her couch was Tilly Bell, Terra, and….

"What have you done?" Avery choked out in alarm.

It looked like her vacation was over. Avery's gaze moved from RITA2 to DAR. She shaded her eyes a bit as she rubbed her brow. The damn hologram was glowing so brightly that he hurt her eyes. She looked more closely at the little ones on the couch.

"Cosmos, Tilly, will one of you please tell me how in the hell a computer program can have babies?!" she growled.

To be continued: Saving Runt: Cosmos' Gateway Book 7

From the shadows of the computer world, Amelia 'Runt' Thomas plays a cat and mouse game with the most ruthless criminals in the world, but her life takes an unexpected turn when she encounters Derik 'Tag Krell Manok— an alien warrior from another world….

EXPERIENCE THE STORIES

If you loved this story by me (S.E. Smith) please leave a review! You can also take a look at additional books and sign up for my newsletter to hear about my latest releases at:

http://sesmithfl.com
http://sesmithya.com

or keep in touch using the following links:

http://sesmithfl.com/?s=newsletter
https://www.facebook.com/se.smith.5
https://twitter.com/sesmithfl
http://www.pinterest.com/sesmithfl/
http://sesmithfl.com/blog/
http://www.sesmithromance.com/forum/

The Full Booklist

Science Fiction / Romance

Dragon Lords of Valdier Series

It all started with a king who crashed on Earth, desperately hurt. He inadvertently discovered a species that would save his own.

Abducting Abby (Book 1)
Capturing Cara (Book 2)
Tracking Trisha (Book 3)
Dragon Lords of Valdier Boxset Books 1-3
Ambushing Ariel (Book 4)
For the Love of Tia Novella (Book 4.1)
Cornering Carmen (Book 5)
Paul's Pursuit (Book 6)
Twin Dragons (Book 7)
Jaguin's Love (Book 8)
The Old Dragon of the Mountain's Christmas (Book 9)
Pearl's Dragon Novella (Book 10)
Twin Dragons' Destiny (Book 11)

Curizan Warrior Series

The Curizans have a secret, kept even from their closest allies, but even they are not immune to the draw of a little known species from an isolated planet called Earth.

Ha'ven's Song (Book 1)

Marastin Dow Warriors Series

The Marastin Dow are reviled and feared for their ruthlessness, but not all want to live a life of murder. Some wait for just the right time to escape....

A Warrior's Heart Novella

Sarafin Warriors Series

The St. Claire family may be slightly ridiculous, but they are formidable. Those cat-shifting aliens won't know what hit them!

Choosing Riley (Book 1)
Viper's Defiant Mate (Book 2)
Heart of the Cat (Book 3)

Dragonlings of Valdier Novellas

The Valdier, Sarafin, and Curizan Lords had children who just cannot stop getting into trouble! There is nothing as cute or funny as magical, shapeshifting kids, and nothing as heartwarming as family.

A Dragonling's Easter
A Dragonling's Haunted Halloween
A Dragonling's Magical Christmas
The Dragonlings' Very Special Valentine
Night of the Demented Symbiots (Halloween 2)
The Dragonlings and the Magic Four-Leaf Clover

Cosmos' Gateway Series

Cosmos created a portal between his lab and the warriors of Prime. Discover new worlds, new species, and outrageous adventures as secrets are unravelled and bridges are crossed.

Tilly Gets Her Man (Prequel)
Tink's Neverland (Book 1)
Hannah's Warrior (Book 2)
Tansy's Titan (Book 3)
Cosmos' Promise (Book 4)
Merrick's Maiden (Book 5)
Core's Attack (Book 6)
Saving Runt (Book 7)

The Alliance Series

When Earth received its first visitors from space, the planet was thrown into a panicked chaos. The Trivators came to bring Earth into the Alliance of Star Systems, but now they have been forced to take control of Earth to prevent the humans from destroying it in their fear, and to protect them from the militant forces of other worlds. No one was prepared for how the humans will affect the Trivators, though, starting with a family of three sisters....

Hunter's Claim (Book 1)
Razor's Traitorous Heart (Book 2)
Dagger's Hope (Book 3)
The Alliance Boxset Books 1-3

Challenging Saber (Book 4)
Destin's Hold (Book 5)
Edge of Insanity (Book 6)
The Alliance Boxset Books 1-6

Lords of Kassis Series
It began with a random abduction and a stowaway, and yet, somehow, the Kassisans knew the humans were coming long before now. The fate of more than one world hangs in the balance, and time is not always linear....
River's Run (Book 1)
Star's Storm (Book 2)
Jo's Journey (Book 3)
Rescuing Mattie Novella (Book 3.1)
Ristéard's Unwilling Empress (Book 4)

Zion Warriors Series
Time travel, epic heroics, and love beyond measure. Sci-fi adventures with heart and soul, laughter, and awe-inspiring discovery...
Gracie's Touch (Book 1)
Krac's Firebrand (Book 2)

Science Fiction / Paranormal / Fantasy / Romance

Magic, New Mexico Series
Within New Mexico is a small town named Magic, an... unusual town, to say the least. With no beginning and no end, spanning genres, authors, and universes, hilarity and drama combine to keep you on the edge of your seat!
Touch of Frost (Book 1)
Taking on Tory (Book 2)
Alexandru's Kiss (Book 3)
Magic, New Mexico Boxset Books 1-3

Paranormal / Fantasy / Romance

Spirit Pass Series

There is a physical connection between two times. Follow the stories of those who travel back and forth. These westerns are as wild as they come!
Indiana Wild (Book 1)
Spirit Warrior (Book 2)

Second Chance Series
Stand-alone worlds featuring a woman who remembers her own death. Fiery and mysterious, these books will steal your heart.
Lily's Cowboys
Touching Rune

More Than Human Series
Long ago there was a war on Earth between shifters and humans. Humans lost, and today they know they will become extinct if something is not done....
Ella and the Beast (Book 1)

The Fairy Tale Series
A twist on your favorite fairy tales!
The Beast Prince Novella
*Free Audiobook of The Beast Prince is available:
https://soundcloud.com/sesmithfl/sets/the-beast-prince-the-fairy-tale-series

The Seven Kingdoms
Long ago, a strange entity came to the Seven Kingdoms to conquer and feed on their life force. It found a host, and she battled it within her body for centuries while destruction and devastation surrounded her. Our story begins when the end is near, and a portal is opened....
The Dragon's Treasure (Book 1)
The Sea King's Lady (Book 2)
A Witch's Touch (Book 3)
The Sea Witch's Redemption (Book 4)

Epic Science Fiction / Action Adventure

Project Gliese 581G Series

An international team leave Earth to investigate a mysterious object in our solar system that was clearly made by someone, *someone who isn't from Earth. Sometimes we truly are too curious for our own good. Discover new worlds and conflicts in a sci-fi adventure sure to become your favorite!*

Command Decision (Book 1)
First Awakenings (Book 2)
Survivor Skills (Book 3)

New Adult / Young Adult

Breaking Free Series

Makayla steals her grandfather's sailboat and embarks on a journey that will challenge everything she has ever believed about herself.

Voyage of the Defiance
Capture of the Defiance

Makayla is older now, but when she needs help, her friends from years ago join new and unexpected allies. Capture of the Defiance is a thriller mystery that stands on its own as danger reveals itself in sudden, heart-stopping moments.

The Dust Series

Fragments of a comet hit Earth, and Dust wakes to discover the world as he knew it is gone. It isn't the only thing that has changed, though, so has Dust...

Dust: Before and After (Book 1)
Dust: A New World Order (Book 2)

Recommended Reading Order Lists:

http://sesmithfl.com/reading-list-by-events/
http://sesmithfl.com/reading-list-by-series/

ABOUT THE AUTHOR

S.E. Smith is an ***internationally acclaimed, New York Times* and *USA TODAY Bestselling*** author of science fiction, romance, fantasy, paranormal, and contemporary works for adults, young adults, and children. She enjoys writing a wide variety of genres that pull her readers into worlds that take them away.

49628461R00114

Made in the USA
Columbia, SC
25 January 2019